Vendetta

FERN MICHAELS

WHEELER PUBLISHING

Published in 2006 by arrangement with Zebra Books, an imprint of
Kensington Publishing Corp.

Wheeler Large Print Softcover.

The text of this Large Print edition is unabridged.
Other aspects of the book may vary from the original edition.

Set in 16 pt. Plantin by Christina S. Huff.

Printed in the United States on permanent paper.

Library of Congress Cataloging-in-Publication Data

Michaels, Fern.
    Vendetta / by Fern Michaels.
      p.   cm. — (Sisterhood ; #4)
    ISBN 1-59722-274-7 (lg. print : sc : alk. paper)
    1. Revenge — Fiction.   2. Female friendship — Fiction.
   3. Victims of crimes — Fiction.   4. Large type books.   I. Title.
   II. Series: Michaels, Fern. Sisterhood ; bk. 4.
   PS3563.I27V46 2006
   813'.54—dc22   2006009875

Vendetta

Prologue

Myra Rutledge's eyes snapped open but she lay still so as not to wake Charles. Gradually she inched her way to the far side of the bed. She looked over at Charles to see if she'd disturbed him. His breathing was deep and even. Satisfied, she slipped out of bed.

Today was her day. For five years she'd waited for this day, longed for it, even lusted after it. In less than twelve hours it would finally be in her grasp. A smile tugged at the corners of her mouth. Like one could really grasp hold of a day!

Myra glanced behind her to make sure Charles was still sleeping soundly before she pulled on her robe and padded downstairs. The first thing she did was turn the thermostat to eighty degrees. Shivering inside her fleece-lined robe, she hugged her arms across her chest. Although the farmhouse she lived in was old, the heating unit was modern, recently installed, and top of the range. She knew the kitchen would heat up in just minutes.

The moment Myra felt the warm air circle around her ankles she made her way to the counter to make a pot of coffee. This was her special time, this early part of the day when the sun was just about to creep over the horizon. It was a brand new day in which anything could happen.

She sat down in an old cane-backed chair with red checkered cushions to wait for the coffee to finish dripping. She noticed that her hands were trembling. Without thinking, she sat on them to stop the shaking. Too bad she couldn't sit on her entire body; she was shaking all over.

Myra could hardly believe that, later today, the Sisterhood — the secret organization she had started after her daughter Barbara was killed by a diplomat's son — would convene once again in the secret room beneath the old house.

Within hours of the hit-and-run accident that killed Barbara and the child she carried, the young driver was whisked out of the country, leaving Myra to grieve and die a little each day. She'd had no recourse for retribution.

Until now.

She got up, poured some coffee and carried it back to the table. She'd done this exact same thing hundreds of times over the past few years, drinking her coffee and reliving her daughter's tragic death . . .

Myra had turned sixty that day and they were celebrating at the Jockey Club in Washington, D.C. It had been her restaurant of choice. She'd been the first to arrive and had allowed Franklin to seat her party in the smoking section; back then you could still smoke in restaurants. Not that she or her two girls smoked; they'd given up the ugly habit, but on special occasions they still had a cigarette with a drink.

She remembered being thrilled at Barbara and Nikki's idea to celebrate with just the three of them. Not even Charles had been included. He had grumbled a bit, but he understood about Girls' Night. God alone knew how much she loved those two girls. She'd adopted Nikki at a young age, but she couldn't love her more if she was her own flesh and blood.

It had started out such a wonderful evening, with Barbara confiding that not only was she getting married, but that she was pregnant as well. She wanted to get married in the living room at Pinewood so she could slide down the bannister in her wedding gown. What was it she'd said? "If I can't do that, the wedding is off." Myra had promised to catch her at the bottom. How they'd all laughed at that image.

"We need pictures of this celebration," Barbara had said. She remembered that Nikki had a camera in the trunk of her car, and before anyone could object, she was up and out of the restaurant and running across the street. Myra and Nikki had smiled as they watched her from their table by the window.

And then the unthinkable happened. Barbara looked up, waved at them and started across the street. The car bearing diplomatic plates came from out of no-where. A second later Barbara was sprawled on the road, cars screeching, people screaming, and then the police and the ambulance arrived.

And that was the end of Myra's world as she knew it.

Myra sipped at her lukewarm coffee. This part of her reverie was where she always floundered. The year following Barbara's death was a total blank. Some-how she'd survived, first with Charles's and Nikki's help, and then by seeing a CNN news report. A woman named Marie Lewellen had taken the law into her own hands when the justice system failed to convict the man who raped and killed her only daughter. Right there on the courthouse steps, with the whole world watching, Marie Lewellen had pulled out a gun and shot her daughter's killer. Myra then hired Nikki to defend Marie Lewellen. Nikki's fiancé, Jack Emery, was the prosecutor. Even though they were engaged and on opposite sides of the fence, Nikki took the case — much to her fiancé's chagrin.

Myra had posted a million-dollar bail for Marie so that she could be at home with her family. Knowing in her heart and gut that Marie would be convicted, she'd asked Charles to help her whisk the entire family to safety. With Charles's expertise from his background as a covert operative for Her Majesty in MI6, they had successfully hidden the Lewellen family. To this day, their disappearance was still a mystery to anyone who cared enough to inquire.

So yes, Myra was out a million dollars, but in her opinion, it was the best million dollars she'd ever spent. What did bother her was how relentless Jack Emery had become and how determined he was to get to the bottom of what he called "Myra's duplicity." Because of his zeal, Nikki eventually broke off their engagement, and she and Jack were now bitter, angry adversaries.

Myra got up to refill her coffee mug and saw Charles standing in the doorway. She rushed over to hug him. He gathered her close to kiss her cheek.

"Is it a good morning, Myra?"

"The best, Charles, the very best. I was just sitting here thinking and remembering." At the look of concern in his eyes, she hastened to add, "I know, I know, but I wasn't *dwelling* on the past. Remembering is all right. I don't ever want to forget, but I can handle it now. Sit down, dear, and let me get you some coffee. I just love this time of day when it's only the two of us . . . Oh, we're getting old, aren't we?"

Charles's eyes twinkled. "A little, but that's not something we're going to think about. It's how we *feel* that's important. It will be so good to see our girls again. I have everything ready."

Myra set the coffee cup in front of Charles. "Do you . . . do you ever regret letting me talk you into forming the Sisterhood?"

"Not one little bit. I do miss my days in Her Majesty's service, but what we're doing here with the girls makes me miss it

12

less and less. It gives me a chance to renew old acquaintances, to ask for their specialized help. Make no mistake, Myra, without your money we could never do what we're doing."

"Charles, let's be fair. We each bring something to the Sisterhood. Your expertise, my money, Nikki's legal abilities, Kathryn's eighteen-wheeler, Alexis's red bag of tricks, Julia's surgical skills, Isabelle's architectural expertise, and of course, Yoko's Eastern philosophies. Oh, and let us not forget Murphy, whose superior canine instincts warn us when Jack Emery is getting a little too close for comfort." She paused. "I told you when we started the Sisterhood that I would gladly give up every cent I owned to get justice for Barbara. I meant every word of it back then and I still mean every word of it today . . . Are we ready for the girls' arrival?"

"We are on target, Myra. This is . . . What does Kathryn call it? Oh, yes, your gig. The big question is, are you ready at last to get the justice that was denied you when Barbara's killer returned to his own country?"

"Charles, I am *so* ready. I couldn't sleep all night just thinking about it. I can't wait

13

to see the girls again. It's been a few months. Phone calls and emails aren't enough, but you're right, the less they come out here, the better. I wonder if Nikki has any news on Jack and his partner. Oh, we have so much to catch up on. It's a wonderful day, isn't it? I said that already, didn't I? I'm just excited, over-whelmed. I thought this day would never come and here it is, right in our faces."

"Yes. Even though it's only forty-two de-grees outside. It is toasty in here, though. So toasty warm I'm thinking we should go upstairs and take a shower together. When was the last time we did that?" Charles led the way to the stairs.

Myra doubled over laughing. "Yester-day."

"Way to go, Mom!"

Myra whirled around, her eyes wide. "Barbara!"

"Yeah. Just stopped in for a little visit. I miss Willie. This is the big day, Mom. I wanted to wish you luck. Go get 'em, tiger. You better hurry, Charles is waiting for you."

"Are you coming, Myra?" Charles called from the top of the stairs.

"I'm coming. I'm coming."

One

Myra walked over to the kitchen door to peer outside. She eyed the temperature gauge and gasped. "Charles, it's twenty-seven degrees! Good heavens! Do we have enough wood for all the fireplaces? We did have an oil delivery, didn't we? We're going to freeze down in the war room."

"Darling, relax. We have two full cords of wood. I carried several loads in earlier this afternoon. Oil was delivered three days ago. We are not going to freeze. Don't you remember, dear, we had special heaters installed in the war room in early September?"

"You're right, I forgot. I am just so overwhelmed that I am finally. . . . Never mind, it's all I've been talking about today. Your ears must be sore by now. The girls are late, aren't they?"

"No, Myra, the girls are not late. We said seven and it's only six-thirty. Please try and relax. Do you think they will like my dinner? I thought about doing something fancy and elegant but decided, that, with the weather, the girls might like some comfort food. And I know how you like my pot roast."

"It smells wonderful, Charles. The potato pancakes are my favorite. We have both sour cream and apple sauce, right?"

Charles wagged his wooden spoon in the air. "I have it all under control, right down to the wine, salad and dessert — and no, I did not forget Murphy."

"Oh, Charles, whatever would I do without you? Never mind, I don't even want to think about that. They're *almost* late."

"Almost doesn't count, my dear." Charles pointed to the security monitor positioned over the back door. "I think they're here now. I see Kathryn's rig in the lead. I think they wait at the end of the road so they can all arrive at the same time."

"I think so, too. One car is missing, Charles. The girls will want to know all about Julia." Myra started to fret again. "It's not going to be the same without her. The empty chair is going to . . . Oh, Charles, I feel like crying."

"There's no time to cry, Myra. I hear

Murphy barking. I think that means he's glad to be back. Open the door, welcome our guests. We'll talk about Julia later."

There were squeals of delight, backslapping, high-fives and hugs galore as the five women and Murphy raced into the kitchen. The jabbering was so high-pitched that Murphy went into the huge family room to lie by the fireplace.

"Oh, I missed you all," Isabelle said happily.

Alexis dumped her red bag by the door and ran to Myra. She hugged her so hard, Myra squealed for mercy. Yoko, always subdued, clapped everyone on the back and then hugged them all. Kathryn ran around the counter to the kitchen window to see if Julia's plant was still there. It was.

"Oh God. Oh God, it has two new leaves! Hey, everyone, Julia's plant has two new leaves! We have to move it, Myra. It's too cold on the windowsill. See how the leaves are limp. Where can I put it? Yoko, you're the plant expert, what should we do?"

The women crowded around to stare at the plant Julia had left behind when she went to Switzerland, hoping to find a cure for her deadly disease. Myra looked stricken, as though she had somehow personally failed their missing sister.

17

Yoko picked up the plant, stuck her finger in the soil and then touched the leaves. "Some light, a little warmer area and it will be fine," she said.

It was finally decided to place the little plant on a small folding table directly under the kitchen skylight. Everyone sighed with relief.

"Any news about Julia?" Nikki asked as she filched a strip of bacon that was to go into the arugula salad. Charles pretended to swat her with his wooden spoon.

"Julia is doing well," Charles said. "She's gained eight pounds in the last four months. She's tolerating her meds and she misses us all terribly. She's coming home for Thanksgiving, and again for Christmas, but then will go back for another six months. What that means is, she's holding her own and she has not regressed or gotten worse. She's happy. She reads, takes walks, rides her bicycle. Her stamina is better than it's ever been. I spoke to her yesterday. She misses you all and she sends her love. She wants you to give Murphy a big hug for her. The first thing she asked about was the plant. To say she was overjoyed at the two new leaves would be putting it mildly." This last comment was addressed to Kathryn, who was busily wiping tears from the corners of her eyes.

"Everything smells wonderful," Nikki said as she carried candles and napkins into the dining room. "Anything new these past few weeks?" she asked Myra.

"Nothing, dear. Charles and I have just been rattling around out here all by ourselves. No one has called or stopped by. Is there any news on Jack?"

"No. That's why I thought . . . I assumed he would. . . . Damn, I don't know what I thought or assumed. I check his and Mark's new Web site daily. I have no clue what the two of them are doing. That could be good or it could be bad."

"I can't believe Jack gave up his job as assistant district attorney, and I can't believe his friend would give up his job as a federal agent just like that," Isabelle said.

"Well, he did." Nikki clicked a lighter to light the scented candles. Within seconds the room smelled like blueberries.

"Are we celebrating something special tonight?" Yoko asked.

"Yes. The good news on Julia, your arrival and anything else we want to celebrate," Myra said. "Goodness, how I've missed you all. But before I forget, Charles and I want to invite you all for Thanks-

19

giving, Christmas, and New Year's. Please say you will come."

"You bet," Kathryn said.

"Wouldn't miss it for the world," Alexis said.

"I will be glad to attend," Yoko said. "My husband will spend the day sleeping so he will not miss me."

Isabelle and Nikki smiled and nodded.

"We go out to the woods and chop the tree down," Myra said. "If it snows, we pull the tree on a sled, but if there's no snow we pull it on a wagon. We cut all the evergreens the same day so they'll be fresh. We haven't really celebrated Christmas here at Pinewood for some years now. I think it's time to get back to our traditions."

"Christmas here at Pinewood is a marvel. The house smells heavenly with all the balsam," Nikki said. "The vaulted ceiling allows us to have a twenty-foot high tree and balsam twined around the bannister going all the way to the second floor. Lots of red velvet bows and our own mistletoe. Myra always made it like a fairyland for Barbara and me. One year, Lu Chow, Myra's gardener, played Santa. She thought we wouldn't notice a Chinese Santa. We pretended not to for her sake."

20

"You knew? You little rascal!" Myra said. Nikki laughed.

They could have been simply a group of young people getting together to play catch-up, or a group of old friends enjoying dinner together.

"I had a date!" Kathryn blurted out, her face rosy pink. She looked around the table at the stunned looks.

"Tell me you didn't wear that flannel shirt and those Frye boots," Alexis said.

"No, I didn't wear them. I got dressed up. Panty hose, makeup, the whole magilla."

"And?" the others chorused as one.

"And nothing. Murphy didn't like him. By the end of the evening the guy was all over me. I had to deck him, at which point he got a little pissy with me. He was so good-looking, he made my eyes water. But I won't be seeing him again. Now, don't ask me any questions because I told you the whole thing."

"I had a date, too," Alexis said. "One of the women I shop for fixed me up with her next-door neighbor. Nice guy. He manages La Belle, that new restaurant in D.C. The food was excellent. He asked me out again. I said yes." Everyone clapped their approval.

"I bought a plasma TV," Nikki said.

"I had to get a new transmission for my car," Isabelle said.

"Well, nothing is new in my life," Yoko said. "I ordered two thousand poinsettias for the holidays. With Lu Chow helping us I will be able to get away for your mission, Myra. I owe you many thanks for allowing him to work at odd times for us. My husband likes him very much."

"That leaves you, Charles. Share with us what you've been up to," Kathryn said.

Charles chuckled. "I've been trying to amuse Myra because she missed you all so much. In my free time, I've been working on the details of her mission."

"Guess that means we're all caught up. Let's clear up this mess," Nikki said, waving at the table, "so we can get down to business."

The war room, as they called it, was warm and cozy. Computer monitors lined the walls, along with television monitors tuned to the three major cable networks: CNN, MSNBC, and the Fox network. Directly in the women's line of vision was an oversized monitor showing the scales of justice, with Lady Justice looking down on them.

A soft whirring could be heard above the quiet tones on the televisions. A fortune in the latest high-tech equipment was at Charles's fingertips. Some of the equipment was so advanced even the FBI didn't have it. "Spare no expense, get the best so the girls are kept safe," Myra had said. And Charles had done just that. He was Lord Supreme in this room and everyone knew it.

Myra usually presided over the meetings, but as it was her mission that was to be discussed this evening, Nikki rose and addressed the group. "This is where we all give input after Myra tells us what she wants done to the man who killed Barbara. We all know he's back in China and that's our first hurdle. I personally don't see any way to entice him back here, so that means we have to go there. We'll have to figure out a way to do that, of course. First, though, I think Myra might want to say something. Myra, the floor is yours," Nikki said, sitting down.

Myra stood up, her legs wobbly. She grasped the edge of the table with both hands as she stared around at the women who were now like daughters to her. They were her family and she knew that, no matter what she asked of them, they would do it if humanly possible. How much should she ask of them? Going to a foreign country to seek her vengeance seemed extreme. Still, there really was no other way to punish her daughter's killer. She looked from one to the other, recognizing each one's particular strength. If anyone could help her, it was these five beautiful, talented women, each with her own cause.

Myra licked at her dry lips. "I . . . My quest for justice is going to be dangerous for all of you. I don't know if I have the courage to ask you to . . . to help me. I won't be offended if you want to opt out of my mission. Somehow, someway, I'll get justice for my daughter. What I'm trying to say is, if anything happened to any of you, I wouldn't be able to live with myself. This won't be anything like Kathryn's or Julia's missions.

"You all know Charles's background, and we'll be operating in his field of expertise. But none of you are Charles and none of you are like the operatives he worked with when he was in Her Majesty's service. Right away, that puts us all at a disadvantage."

Kathryn, always the most vocal of the group, squawked her displeasure at what Myra was saying. "Myra, Myra, you're forgetting something. We're *women!* That alone gives us an edge! I rest my case." Everyone cheered, including Charles. Myra grinned from ear to ear.

"Well said, Kathryn. You are forgiven, dear. How stupid of me to forget women can do anything they set their minds to. I think I might be a little overwhelmed at this point. Now, let's decide how we are going to take care of Mr. John Chai, my daughter's killer."

"If Julia was here she could do a little slice and dice with a *very* dull knife. But since she isn't here, I'll volunteer to do the honors, and if he bleeds to death, oh, well," Alexis said.

"That's too good for him. He needs to suffer. His father needs to suffer for protecting him. Let's see what Charles has come up with."

Charles shuffled through the papers in front of him. When he had them in order, images appeared on the screen as Lady Justice faded away. "This is John Chai." A second picture appeared. "This is Chai Ming, China's former Ambassador to the United States. He is retired now and living in Hong Kong. From what I've been able to garner from my sources, Chai Ming has a pretty tight rein on his playboy son."

Charles sought Myra's eye. "I haven't been able to find any evidence of employment of any kind. I would assume he's living off the largesse of his father, Chai Ming. John's Harvard education was a waste."

"Is he still covered under the law of diplomatic immunity even though his father is retired?" Yoko asked.

"Yes, but he cannot return to the United States for fear of reprisals, that sort of thing. It's obvious the man stays close to home under his father's supervision. Sooner or later, he's going to wander off the reservation. It's a given that he will not return here to America. That means we will bring him here. Unwillingly, of course."

The women gasped as one. "You mean we're going to go to China and . . . and . . ."

"Snatch the son of a bitch?" Kathryn said. "Yep, that's what it means all right."

"Tell us how we are going to get inside China, snatch this guy, and get back out," Nikki demanded. "I would think the Chai family are watched as closely as our Secret Service agents watch over our retired politicians."

Charles nodded. "You're right, Nikki, but in China they are watched even more closely. I can't swear to this, but I do know how the Chinese think in these matters. It's doubtful Ming's own eye is on his son. There are hundreds of eyes on him. They don't want any kind of scandal that will make them lose face. Family is very important. Respect of one's family is paramount."

Myra's eyes pooled with tears. "If it's impossible, why are we even discussing the matter? Why was I so foolish to think we could finally get to . . . that . . . hellish person?"

"Myra, dear, it is not impossible to get to John Chai. However, it will be a very dangerous and difficult mission for all of us. We are going to need a lot of outside help."

"What kind of help?" Isabelle asked nervously.

"Chinese help. In . . . ah . . . in my other life, I made friends with some very unlikely people. People that I was forced to depend on to stay alive. One develops, over time, instincts where people are concerned. I have a friend named Su Zhow Li. He got me out of a rather horrid situation and then I was able to save his life later on. He is probably in his mid-seventies by now if he is still alive. I haven't been able to renew old friendships since moving here. That was one of the conditions of my transfer from England to America. I'm now willing to ignore that condition.

"Li was born in China but spent many years living in England. His father was British, his mother came from a very well-to-do Chinese family. In the early fifties, as some of you may know, China undertook a massive economic and social reconstruction program. China's new leaders curbed inflation by restoring the economy, and rebuilt many of its war-damaged industrial plants." It had been years since Li told him this story and Charles wondered if he was remembering everything correctly.

"China's new leaders, with their new-found authority, wedged their way into almost every phase of Chinese life. It worked for a few years, then Mao Zedong, founder of the People's Republic, broke away from the Soviet model of Communism and announced what he thought of as an even better economic system. They called it the Great Leap Forward. The goal was to raise industrial and agricultural production. They formed communes. People had factories in their back yards. It was disastrous because the normal market mechanisms were disrupted and so agricultural production fell behind. The Chinese people exhausted themselves by producing what later turned out to be shoddy goods that were not fit for sale."

"Tell me about it," Yoko grumbled. "I wouldn't buy something that said 'made in China' for all the tea in China." She giggled at her witticism.

"Bad timing, poor planning, whatever you want to call it, the Chinese people were starving. Around this time, Li's family sought passage to his homeland."

Charles knew he'd piqued the women's interest when Kathryn asked, "How did they manage to get out of China?"

Charles grinned wryly. "Very carefully, that's how. Li never gave me all the details, but he did say it was a long, dangerous journey. Li's mother had connections and money. They finally arrived in England and amassed a fortune in silks. Li was sent to America and graduated from Harvard at the top of his class. He is a brilliant man. Years and years later, he returned to Hong Kong a very wealthy man."

"Is he going to help us?" Nikki asked.

"Patience, my dear, patience," Charles said.

Myra banged her clenched fist on the table. "I have no patience, Charles. Please, get to the point. Do you have a plan?" Her tone of voice said quite clearly that Charles had better have a plan.

Evidently Charles thought so, too. "The reason I brought up my old friend Li is because he has a private airstrip outside of Hong Kong."

The silence in the room was palpable as the women digested Charles's words. That brought it all front and center. They were going to China.

"I'm waiting for Li to contact me via a scrambled phone. I'll have more details as soon as I hear from him." Charles looked around from one to the other. They all looked worried, except Myra who was smiling serenely. "This . . . caper . . . will test your skills to the fullest."

"Like hacking off the balls of three guys didn't take skill!" Kathryn hooted, referring to their first mission. The others clapped their hands in agreement. "And let's not forget those creeps we just sent off to Africa. Skill is knowing what to do at precisely the right moment. As women, we have a honed instinct that allows us to improvise in a heartbeat."

The women clapped again. Myra clapped the loudest, her eyes bright and shiny.

Two

It was a storefront office nestled between a Blockbuster video store and a Radio Shack in a strip mall in McLean, Virginia. The sign was a simple brass plate with black lettering that said JUSTICE AGENCY. The door was locked, the blinds closed.

The hour was late, way past the Justice Agency's normal closing hour, which was any time of the day or night. Tonight was an exceptionally late night because neither Jack Emery nor Mark Lane was in a hurry to brave the cold outside and return to the apartment they shared to cut down on expenses. Both men had their feet propped on their desks as they sipped at their beer.

"This private dick business isn't so bad," Mark said. "We made eight thousand, six hundred dollars in the last six weeks. What that means is we get a nice little bonus this week. We have two prospective clients who are sitting on the fence. I think we're doing damn good for just getting started in the

31

business. Hell, Jack, with all these programs I installed on our computers, we hardly have to leave the office. Our biggest expense is those guys we hired to tail your buddies out at ye olde Pinewood farm."

Jack swigged from his beer bottle. His feet thumped down on the floor. "Five months and there's been no word on Senator Webster or his wife, Dr. Webster. No one but Nikki has gone near the farm. That's the same MO they used when Marie Lewellen disappeared on my watch. They lie low, let the smoke settle, and then those damn women spring up like jack-in-the-boxes."

"They were all at the farm today except for Dr. Webster," Mark said.

"What? You're just telling me this now?" Jack exploded.

"Look, hot shot, it came just this minute in this email. Garrity is reporting in. All of them except Dr. Webster got there around seven o'clock. It's almost midnight and they're still there. Guess they're going to spend the night. Garrity says the house is dark."

"Son of a bitch! Didn't I tell you? They lie low, wait four or five months, and then they meet up. Then . . . then they do *something*. Right this damn minute they're in there hatching and planning. I know it! I feel it! We have to figure out a way to plant some bugs in that house."

"Forget it. Those Dobermans are still out there and there's no way I'm messing with that guy Charles Martin. You want another visit from those guys with the shields?" Mark winced, remembering the elite presidential task force that had beaten Jack within an inch of his life for interfering with Charles Martin.

Jack ignored the rhetorical question as he looked across his desk at his friend, the ex-FBI agent. "Something has been bothering me for a long time now. I couldn't get a handle on it. It was something I knew I should remember but couldn't, that kind of thing. I finally remembered it, Mark. There *is* a way into Pinewood."

Mark grimaced. "Don't go there, Jack. Please."

"No, no. Listen. The tunnels. That's our way in and out. Nikki and Barbara used to play in the tunnels when they were children. Nikki told me that Myra hung bells at the different intersections so they wouldn't get lost. In the old days they used to spirit out the slaves to a safe place by way of the tunnels. Nikki said there was an exit in the barn and one tunnel that went all the way to some other farmhouse. I can't remember which house it was, though. I can't be sure, but I think she said the other people closed their section off. Shit, I wish I could remember exactly what she said. If we can figure it out, we can get in that way."

Mark stared at a seascape hanging on the wall across the room. "What's with that *we* stuff? I'm not crawling through any two-hundred-year-old tunnels. I'm strictly a computer nerd who's willing to do surveillance from time to time. In addition, I'm claustrophobic. You're nuts, Jack!"

"Yeah, well, if you can come up with a better way to get inside, I'm all ears. We're just spinning our wheels here. If we can't get inside we might as well give it all up. I'm not willing to do that. I know I'm right about those women. You know I'm right about those women. Those guys who beat me up know I'm on to something where those chicks are concerned, otherwise they wouldn't have threatened me and then almost killed me. I'm willing to do the breaking and entering. I just need you to cover my ass."

"I can do that. Cover your ass, I mean."

"Good. Now, before we leave, see if you can find out the best way to tranquilize those Dobermans. We'll need to post Garrity out there on a permanent basis so he can tell us when everyone is out of the house. Don't look at me like that, Mark, it's all doable. I'm the one who will do it. This is it. I can feel it in my bones. Yahoo!"

"Yeah, yahoo," Mark said, clicking at the keys in front of him.

Five miles away, even though the house was totally dark, the war room was alight not only with wattage, but also with smiles and hope.

Charles walked among the women, handing out packets of information. "I want you all to familiarize yourselves with China. I want you to understand the people, the customs and the terrain. I'm going to say this once and then I won't mention it again. If any one of you feels this is above and beyond what you've all signed up to do, you can withdraw now and none of us here will hold it against you." He waited for a response. What he got was a group nod, which meant that they were all *in* and no one wanted *out*.

They jumped as one when Charles's encrypted phone rang. No one seemed surprised when Charles carried on his end of the conversation in Chinese. He truly was a man of many talents. All eyes were on Yoko to see if she was following the conversation. She was. She nodded from time to time before she held her thumb upright. She whispered in English, "We're going. He will allow us to use his airstrip. They are making plans now."

"Oh, this is so wonderful. I can't think of anything to say," Myra bubbled.

When Charles ended his call, he approached the sisters, the light of battle in his eyes. "We have a deal with Li, ladies. You leave for China tomorrow afternoon. Li will clear the way for us. That's all I'm going to say at the moment. In the morning, I'll have a plan all worked out. It's late, get a good night's rest. We'll meet up again in the morning."

Myra stayed behind, her face puckered with worry. "The deal, Charles — will it keep the girls safe?"

Charles looked down into the eyes of the woman he'd loved all his life. He could no more tell her a lie than he could stop breathing. "I don't know, Myra. Li is an honorable man. I believe he will do everything in his power to make things right for us. It's the best I can do, my darling. The girls are willing to take the risk."

"I think we should go with them, Charles. At least I want to go."

"Out of the question. No, Myra, I mean it. No is no."

"I think I'll go anyway. Goodnight, Charles. Oh, I mean it, too."

The following morning Charles Martin, the man of many talents, looked at the skimpy breakfast he was setting out for Myra's guests. He almost felt ashamed. Almost.

The small group trickled into the kitchen, where they all looked at the toasted muffins, sliced oranges and bananas, juice and coffee. They didn't say a word as they picked up their paper plates and paper napkins. Charles apologized for the meager fare and throwaway dishes. No one seemed to care, even Myra, who was a stickler for a well-set table and fine food. Lunch, Charles explained, was going to be worse. Bologna and cheese sandwiches. Maybe some pickles and chips if they had them. The women did groan about that.

"Eat up, ladies. We'll meet in the war room in exactly," he looked at his watch — "twenty-five minutes." Then he was gone. Murphy barked at this strange behavior. He continued to bark, wondering where the bacon was, his share of the pancakes, or the eggs everyone usually slipped him. Kathryn refused to feed him dog food, saying he ate what she ate. Murphy even liked beer and could belch with the best of them.

"Did you all read up on China?" Nikki asked as she rubbed her temples. She'd had a horrible night, her sleep invaded by dreams of Jack Emery. Even a late-night visit from Barbara couldn't calm her down. There had been no time this morning to cover the dark circles under her eyes. She hoped the others didn't notice.

"We're not all going to China, are we?" Kathryn asked.

Nikki shrugged. "Charles said he was going to work on that through the night. It's his decision, but if you want my guess, I don't think we're all going."

"Well, I'm going," Myra said firmly. "I've waited too long for this moment to sit on the sidelines."

Isabelle got up and looked around. She looked at her watch. "No time to clear this away, our twenty-five minutes are up. Come on, let's go, troops!"

Outside, across the vast lawn covered with frost, and high in one of the old oaks, a man named Garrity brought his high-powered binoculars to his eyes and whistled softly. He could see into Myra Rutledge's kitchen so clearly, he could have been a few feet away. He watched the scrambling exit and frowned. Where the hell were they all going in such a hurry? The old gent had left earlier while the women ate. There had been no sign of him since. With nothing else to occupy him, Garrity crunched down on a granola bar — his breakfast. He pulled out his cell phone when he'd finished the crunchy bar and called Jack Emery. His report was simple. The Dobermans had been picked up, the women had eaten and then disappeared. He was told to sit it out even though he said he was freezing his ass off. Emery promised him time and a half to stay. Garrity agreed.

In the war room, all hell was breaking loose. Charles looked flustered while the women could only stare at Myra, their eyes big, their jaws slack, as she went into a tirade.

"I'm going, and that's final. Don't think for one minute that I am going to stay here worrying. I've waited too long for this moment. For you to think I would be content to sit here on . . . on . . . my ass while you all do my dirty work is unthinkable. Do not make me angry, Charles. I'm not a nice person when I'm angry. Did you hear me? I'm going and that's final. Girls, tell him I'm going!"

The women looked at one another and then at Charles, hoping for him to intervene.

"Myra, listen to me," Charles said. "You cannot go. The reason you cannot go is because of Jack Emery. You need to remain here to keep up appearances. It's crucial. We are going to bring John Chai to you. If you want, we'll wrap him in gold ribbon when we hand-deliver him.

"Yesterday you said we were getting old. That means our reflexes are off. We're slow, we don't think as fast as we have in the past, and we don't move as fast either. It's the way it has to be, Myra. If you insist, then you'll leave me no other recourse than to cancel this mission."

"But . . ."

"There are no buts, Myra. Unintentionally, you could make a mistake and put the girls in danger. I know you don't want that to happen."

"Charles is right, Myra," Nikki said. The others agreed.

Myra seethed. She had the last word though. "This *sucks*, Charles."

Charles turned away to hide his smile. The battle was over and he'd won this round. He turned around again before he flipped a switch. An airstrip appeared on the large screen, followed by a picture of Li's home. More pictures followed — the grounds of Li's estate, the floor plan of the house, and then pictures of the servants. He pressed another button and the pictures printed out. He passed them to Nikki, who handed them to the others.

"Nikki, Yoko, Alexis and I will be going to China. Isabelle will stay here at Pinewood with Myra but will go back and forth to the city for a few hours each day. Kathryn has a delivery of Christmas trees scheduled. She'll be going to Oregon and from Oregon to Delaware."

Yoko looked excited but agitated. "How long will we be away? I need to tell my husband . . ."

"If things go right, it's going to be a smash and grab. That means in and out. Not counting the travel time, five days tops. If things go awry, we'll just have to . . . ah . . . wing it."

"When do we leave?" Nikki asked briskly.

Charles looked at his watch. "In five hours."

"Five hours!" Alexis bellowed. "It will

take me that long to pack up my red bag, not to mention my own personal bag."

"Then I suggest you get a move on. Ladies, we'll meet up in the kitchen in five hours. Run along, I have some last-minute details to take care of."

Jack Emery's cell phone rang at twelve minutes past two in the afternoon. He barked a greeting. "Garrity! I hope you have some good news."

"Good news, bad news, who the hell knows? What I do know is my dick is frozen. How much longer do I have to stay up in this goddamn tree?"

"Till I tell you to come down. I stayed up there for four whole days. If I could do it, so can you. Think about warm, sandy beaches, golden sunshine. What's happening?"

"OK, they all come barreling back into the kitchen an hour after they split. They go off in all directions. Then nothing until just now. Three women and the gent pile into one of those big black, Chevy Suburbans. They had luggage. It was the black girl, your old girlfriend, the Asian girl, and that guy Charles. He drove, by the way. The big rig is still there and so is the architect's car. Mrs Rutledge is inside."

"I suppose it's too much to hope that you picked up some conversation?"

"You're right, Jack, that's too much to hope for. If your next question is where are they going, I'd say an airport, but then again they could be headed for Union Station in D.C. I called Dennison and he said he'd start tailing the Suburban as soon as they hit the highway."

"OK, stay on it. Call me as soon as there's any movement at the farm."

Jack's phone rang almost immediately when he ended his call with Garrity.

"It's me, boss, Dennison. I'm on the Suburban. I think they're headed for Baltimore-Washington Airport."

"Call me back as soon as you know for certain. That's where Myra Rutledge keeps the company Gulfstream. I want to know where they're going, Dennison."

The call over, Jack huddled with Mark. "Things are moving, buddy. Told you this was their MO."

Three

The passengers were jolted awake as the Gulfstream's wheels hit the runway. They looked at one another. Their eyes said *We're in China!*

Charles looked down at his watch. With the eight-hour time difference plus the sixteen-hour flight, he calculated that they were a day behind in Hong Kong. Not that it mattered. At this moment, time was not their problem. Later, time, right down to the nanosecond, could become a deadly enemy. Thank God for Li's help, which had cut through all the bureaucratic red tape. Even the pilot was one of Li's men. Somehow he would find a way to make this all up to Li.

It had been years since he'd been in China. He had never thought he would return, especially under these unusual circumstances. He gazed out the window as the aircraft taxied to a complete stop. The countryside was lush, verdant, just as he

44

remembered. Li had said he lived in the middle of nowhere. This certainly looked like nowhere. All he could see was a sea of green — hundreds, maybe thousands of trees, grass as high as he was tall, and the occasional shimmer of what he assumed to be small ponds as far as the eye could see.

Yoko unbuckled her seatbelt. "I love the countryside. It is beautiful, this place called Hong Kong."

"Actually," Charles said, "we're on a small island outside Hong Kong. It's called Po Toi Island. Li only lives here for part of the year. He's in residence now with a full staff that will be at our disposal. Li understands that this is a very discreet operation and all his people, he assured me, can be trusted."

The little group waited patiently while the ground crew assisted the pilot and co-pilot as they prepared to lower the air stair door.

On the ground, her legs wobbly from sitting so long, Nikki looked back at Myra's luxurious Gulfstream. She'd felt safe sitting in the buttery-soft leather reclining seats, each equipped with a satellite television and phone. Each seat contained a laptop computer and a global positioning sensor. At any given point during the trip they could view what part of the world the aircraft was flying over. A stocked kitchen and bar provided enough food and drink to sustain twelve passengers and a crew for at least several days. And of course there were bowls and bowls of the famous Rutledge candies everywhere.

The Gulfstream was safe. Standing here on the ground in the bright sunshine, Nikki realized she no longer felt safe.

China! She shivered. She took one last, longing look at the Gulfstream, wondering if she and the others would ever set foot in it again. She shivered again as she gave herself a mental warning not to think about negatives.

"I do believe this may be our ride," Charles said, pointing to a gleaming black Lincoln Navigator coming across the tarmac. The driver leaped out of the SUV with the agility of a cat. He had to be at least seventy years of age, possibly older. A mini man, Nikki thought. He was as brown and wrinkled as a raisin. He offered up a toothless smile and then saluted smartly.

Charles rattled off something in fluent Chinese. The old man bowed and climbed behind the wheel as the women scrambled into the back seat, Charles into the passenger seat beside the small man who said his name was Jialing.

"So named after the river. Mr. Li calls me Jay and you may also call me Jay."

Charles and Jay kept up a conversation as they traveled down a rutted road. "What are they saying?" Nikki hissed to Yoko.

"They are talking about how important Mr. Li is in this country. Jay is saying Mr. Li has important, influential friends. He is now saying Mr. Li is a generous man and helps the needy. Jay has been in service to him for thirty years. They are now talking about the fabulous gardens at Mr. Li's home. Mr. Li likes to garden and has beautiful roses. The rooms at his home are full of flowers all the time. How do you call it, chitter-chatting. Nothing of importance," Yoko whispered.

"I suppose that's a good thing," Alexis said quietly.

Thirty minutes later Jay announced they were on Mr. Li's land. "The main house is just down the road," he said.

The women were grateful to finally climb out of the Navigator. The roads here were worse than the roads in the States after a hard winter.

They saw a two-story redbrick house with jutting wings at each side of the building. A British house. Did that mean only tea would be served? Nikki wondered. She needed coffee and she needed it badly.

"If you want my opinion," Alexis said, "this house looks as though it was accidentally built in the wrong place. You know, like Dorothy's house when it landed in Oz. Oops, Dorothy landed in Oz, not the house. You know what I mean — look how out of place it is with the gardens."

"The Chinese do not believe in alignment or symmetrical relationship to anything in the garden simply because they know this is foreign to Mother Nature. They like to copy nature as much as possible with small hills and slopes with different trees. To us it looks haphazard but I'd bet Alexis's red bag that a lot of work and thought went into these gardens."

"I love it. Just look at all the little waterfalls, the small bridges and those gorgeous shrubs. Before I leave here I want to know the name of every one of those trees and bushes. Someday when I get my own house, I'm going to have a garden like this."

"Much work," Yoko said, shaking her head. "Much maintenance."

Alexis sighed. "Don't rain on my parade, Yoko. As you can see, I don't have an umbrella."

Yoko tittered behind her hand. "So funny. No umbrella. So funny."

Suddenly the bright, yellow door of the house opened and a tall, stoop-shouldered man stepped forward. "As I live and breathe, it is you, Sir . . ." He debated a second before he said, "Charles. On my shores at last. It is good to see you, old friend." He bowed slightly before he extended his hand in greeting.

The introductions were made quietly as they all walked into the house, where Li turned the women over to three servants.

Yoko, Alexis, and Nikki looked at one another at the foot of the stairs before they followed the three maids to the second floor. "This is it, girls. The job starts *now,* and God help us all," Nikki said.

"Yoko, can you ask if they can bring us some hot coffee? Lots and lots of hot coffee. But first I want to take a steaming shower and wash my hair. Then I just want to sit and drink all that coffee for ten minutes."

"But of course, Nikki."

Below stairs, the tall man known as Li ushered Charles into his private office. "We will speak English from here on, Charles. While I trust my servants, one can never be too careful, as you well know. Whiskey?"

"Of course." Charles looked around the large, pleasant room. It had everything a man of Li's stature needed. The room appeared to be divided into three parts. There was an entertainment area where a large plasma television and DVD player was attached to the wall. A stereo unit was nestled underneath in a cherrywood cabinet. Off to the side was a fully stocked bar area with four deep, leather swivel chairs and a table holding a glorious flower arrangement. To the right of the bar was what appeared to be Li's work area. Rich, polished wooden file cabinets covered the wall; a comfortable desk chair that looked used sat behind a magnificent carved cherrywood desk. Everything one needed to conduct business from home was on the desk. Paintings with vibrant watercolors dotted the wood-paneled walls that began at the highly polished plank floor and went all the way to the high ceiling.

What surprised Charles more than anything was the absence of window treatments. So Li could look out or so others could look in? He asked his friend.

"One must always be aware in this country, Charles. How would you put it?

The odds are a little more even this way. I spend a great deal of time in this room and, if it should ever become necessary, I can make a hasty exit through the floor. I defy you to find the mechanism that operates the trapdoor. By the way, I crafted it myself. Are you up to the challenge?"

"You're a crafty old fox, I'll give you that. Show me!"

"No. You must find it yourself. We can do it later. I did say I was going to offer you a whiskey, did I not?"

Charles chuckled. "Yes, you did and I am patiently waiting. We must talk, Li. We can socialize later."

Li nodded solemnly. "Tell me everything, Charles, so I can help you. You saved my life once and now it is my turn to help you. You may speak as freely as you wish, but only in English. I personally sweep this room twice a day for . . . ah . . . bugs."

Charles leaned back in his comfortable chair, his whiskey glass in hand. He seemed to have no interest in drinking the amber liquid. He told Li everything. He watched the old man to gauge his reaction.

"Commendable! I applaud you, Charles. From the little you told me on the scrambled phone, I more or less surmised something like this. I personally know John Chai's father. I know *of* John and his unsavory reputation and let me tell you, neither man is on my speed dial. Everything in this country is political, as you well know. Ming is detestable. John is beyond detestable. It gives me great pleasure to help you and perhaps rid this country of such parasites. However, I do not fool myself. Two more will spring up just like them."

"And your safety, Li?"

Li shrugged. "All those I have cared for during my lifetime are gone. I am an old man now. I watch sunrises and sunsets and live with my memories. It is not much of a life these days. Do not worry about me. I always wondered what happened to you. There were, of course, rumors. I did pray for your safety."

Charles allowed himself a small smile. "And I for yours. The old days, Li, are just that, the old days. I see that you have kept up with the times as I have. Do you think that back then we could have functioned in this high-tech world we now live in?"

Li looked around the room and smiled. "I think so, Charles. Now, let us speak of pleasantries. Tell me about the three lovely young ladies upstairs and the thorn in your side named Jack Emery; not that Mr.

Emery is a pleasantry, but perhaps we can arrange it so he *becomes* a pleasantry. In the interests of true love, of course." Charles laughed as Li poured more whiskey into his glass.

A long time later, Li apologized. "You look to me as if a nap is in order. I have been a selfish host wanting to hear everything that has happened in your life. Forgive me. We have all evening to talk." He ushered Charles to the door. A petite woman with coal-black eyes and hair to match appeared out of nowhere to escort Charles to his suite of rooms.

Charles knew the moment the door closed behind him that Li would be working to finalize tomorrow evening's plans. The thought pleased him. They were in safe hands.

The small dinner party took place on a multilayered terrace filled with hundreds of brilliant flowers. The only light came from colored Chinese lanterns. The food was simple but superb: Peking duck, wontons and fresh snow peas. The dessert was rice cakes drizzled with honey and powdered sugar. The wine was American in honor of Li's guests. The conversation was light, almost bantering, as the women asked questions about China. Li in turn asked questions, subtle to be sure, but Nikki knew that she and the others were being grilled by a master. Charles had nodded ever so slightly to assure her it was OK to answer the questions.

It was a warm evening so the girls wore sleeveless sundresses. Charles and Li wore pressed khaki shorts with knee socks, white shirts and ties. It was formal yet informal. The women chatted about the gardens as Charles and Li descended two layers to a terrace below them with brandy and cigars, a courtesy the girls appreciated because they hated cigar smoke.

"Did you see those dresses Mr. Li sent to us? Fantastic," Alexis said.

Yoko agreed. "Do you think I will look good in lavender?"

"Honey, you are going to be a knockout. I'll do your makeup. You will be more beautiful than the . . . What do they call the woman who is getting engaged at the party tomorrow night?"

"Prospective bride, I guess," Nikki said. "I think Charles said she is going to college in the States but came back here to have a traditional Chinese wedding. One old family marrying into another old family. Doting parents on both sides. In other words, the wedding of the year, and not at all unusual to have American guests. Which we are. Perfect cover. Mr. Li is a personal friend of the bride's father and is related to the groom's mother by way of his deceased wife. When Mr. Li told both families he wouldn't be able to attend because we were visiting him, both sets of parents insisted he bring us along. And that's all I know, other than that Mr. Li was able to get all our papers in order lickety-split."

"John Chai is a woman-chaser," Yoko said, her lips tight with anger. "And he prefers American women over . . . over his own kind. I read that in the dossier Charles put together for us."

"I think that lets me and you out, Yoko. You're his kind and I'm black. Guess who that leaves? Oh you lucky, lucky girl, Nikki."

"Shut up, Alexis. How did we get on to this anyway? We were talking about our gowns. Mine is a sizzling red. Tonight I am going to be one hot chick! When, and only when, you see steam coming out my ears, intervene. I think I should play hard to get, don't you?"

"Absolutely!" Yoko said. "Men do not like to be ignored. My husband told me this. It has to do with their ego. This is true, is it not? As a weapon it is wonderful to know. Do you think all women know this?"

"I think so," Nikki replied, thinking about Jack. Jack hated to be ignored. He'd always wanted her undivided attention. When she ignored him, he sulked. "Let me share something with you two. Men are just little boys at heart. And they can be trained just like you train a puppy. You have to be relentless, though, because men/boys have one-track minds. You following me here?" Nikki laughed uproariously.

"What I think is that we've all had too much wine and it's time for bed," Alexis said. "Oh, in case you're all wondering what my gown is like, it's a mix of gold and copper. Slit to the navel, slit up to the groin, and backless!"

"Damn," was all Nikki could say.

Alexis giggled. "My sentiments exactly. C'mon, let's say our goodnights and hit the sheets so we can dream about what we're going to do to John Chai."

"I believe you used the wrong terminology," Yoko said. "The word you want is nightmare."

"Damn, you're good, Yoko. Nightmare it is!" Nikki said as she swallowed the last of many glasses of wine.

Four

Half a world away, as Charles and the girls were dressing for the engagement party in China, Myra Rutledge had her eye on the clock as she paced back and forth in the kitchen.

"Myra, stop! You're making me dizzy. They're fine. Charles isn't going to let anything go wrong."

"I know, I know," Myra said. "My mind tells me the same thing but my heart tells me I should worry. Women have been worrying since the beginning of time. Why should I be any different? They're in China, Kathryn. China is not a safe country."

Kathryn slipped her arms into her flannel-lined denim jacket. Murphy growled and then barked. "I don't like leaving you alone out here at the farm all by yourself, Myra. We should have insisted that Isabelle return this evening. What the hell was so important that she had to stay in the city?"

"I think it was a dinner meeting with someone who can help her get her license back. It's so important to her, how could I say no? I'll be fine. The dogs are here; I'll lock up and wait for Charles or the girls to call me. The minute I hear something, I'll call you. You have enough on your mind without worrying about me."

Something tugged at Kathryn's heart. "I know this is going to sound off the wall, Myra, but how about coming along with me to Oregon? I'll have someone else to talk to besides Murphy. You can ride shotgun with Murphy. Of course you're going to have to get rid of the pearls and all that jewelry hanging off you. You gotta look like me otherwise I'll get drummed out of the trucking business. Think of it as an adventure that you can tell Charles about when he gets home." At Myra's look of disbelief and indecision, Kathryn coaxed her further. "Come on, go for it! When was the last time you did something spontaneously?"

Murphy pulled and tugged at the hem of Myra's knit skirt. He stopped tugging for a moment to look up at his host and bark.

"See! That's Murphy's way of telling you he wants you to come with us. This dog is so smart he makes me crazy sometimes.

Shake it, Myra, we gotta get on the road. Have you ever been to Oregon?"

"Ah, no, dear, I haven't. Do you really . . . Whatever will Charles say?"

Kathryn laughed. "I think he'll say you're a woman of many surprises. We'll have fun. You can talk to some of my road buddies. I'm Big Sis. I can give you a handle. That's what we call a name. You game, lady?"

"You don't think I'm . . . too old to be doing that?"

"Hell, no! Creaking Granny, that's her handle, is seventy-four and she's still driving. You can talk to her when we get on the road."

Myra debated all of five seconds. "OK, I'll do it! But I don't think I have the proper attire. I don't want to . . . to embarrass you, Kathryn."

"We're the same size, Myra. Go up to my room and pick out some duds. Make sure you bring along a baseball cap. All drivers wear baseball caps."

"I can do that. Yes, yes, I can do that. Wait for me." Myra scurried off, Murphy hot on her heels barking every step of the way.

"I'm not going anywhere. Tell you what, I'll warm up the truck. Be sure to put on the alarm and lock up. Leave a note for Isabelle. We can call her in the morning just to be on the safe side. Time is money, Myra! Move!" Kathryn shouted to Myra's retreating back.

Myra got dressed at the speed of light. She looked at herself in the mirror hanging on the door. Her eyebrows shot up to her hairline. "Oh, my goodness! What do you think, Murphy?" The big dog tossed back his head and howled. "Yes, yes, that's pretty much my opinion, too. If Charles could see me now, he'd laugh himself silly."

All Kathryn could do was gawk, her jaw dropping when Myra left the house by the kitchen door. Her thumbs hooked into the belt of her baggy blue jeans, Myra strutted across the compound in her Timberland boots. She was wearing a navy-blue sweat-shirt that said DON'T SCREW WITH ME under a zip-up sleeveless vest with a hood. On her springy gray curls sat a baseball cap that said she was a fan of the Redskins. She wasn't wearing her pearls.

Kathryn bounced out of the truck and went around to open the passenger door.

"This is so exciting. I've never ridden in a truck before. How does one get in this vehicle, Kathryn?"

"I think I'm going to have to boost you up. Right leg up, atta girl!"

Murphy scrambled into the truck, hopped over Myra's shoulder and went to his bed behind the cab. He barked sharply, which meant, "All aboard, let's move!"

Myra buckled up, her eyes sparkling with anticipation. "Dear, this was . . . such a tremendous idea. Ooh, we're up so high! I can see everything."

"You're Queen of the Road today, Myra," Kathryn laughed as she backed up the big rig.

"Is this when you say something profound, like this is where the rubber meets the road?"

"Nah, you only say that when you're about to get in trouble. We say time to hit the road or time to burn rubber . . ."

"I see. Time to hit the road. Burn rubber. I'll be sure to remember that so I can tell Charles. Both sayings refer to speed, I take it."

"You got that right. No one wants to mess with truck drivers. That's the reason for the saying on the shirt you're wearing. I had to earn the right to wear that particular shirt, me being a woman trucker and all. Actually, Creaking Granny gave it to me at the Truckers' Ball three years ago."

"You have a Ball? Is it like a cotillion?"

Kathryn laughed so hard she almost fell off the seat. "Yeah, Myra, like a cotillion." Her sarcasm did not go unnoticed by Myra.

"This is so very interesting. I hope I can remember everything so I can tell Charles. The dear man is going to be stunned. Just stunned."

"Oregon, here we come!" Kathryn said as she blew a wicked blast on the diesel horn.

In the thick pine forest that surrounded the Rutledge house and lawn, Garrity almost fell out of his tree when he heard the diesel blast. In a heartbeat the high-powered binoculars were at his eyes. "What the hell?" he muttered. He continued to watch the eighteen-wheeler until it went through the security gates and out to the main road. He was on his cell phone in the blink of an eye. "Jack, Garrity here. Hey, man, the last two birds just flew the coop. The chick with the eighteen-wheeler took off just minutes ago with her dog and the old lady. Both of them were duded up for a long drive, would be my opinion. There's no one in the house, Jack. Can I go home now?"

"Give me an hour, Garrity. I'm going to need you to cover my ass. I'm coming out there right now. Well, not right now, but as soon as I can get someone to tail that truck. What about the architect? Any sight of her?"

"Nope. She took off earlier. I don't know if this means anything or not but she was carrying an oversize bag and one of those architect's folders. Don't you have someone on her?"

"Mark's got it. I'll check to be sure. Just sit tight till I get there."

"I couldn't move if I wanted to, I'm frozen to this branch. You gotta rotate me out of here, Jack."

"Yeah, yeah, yeah. Stop whining, Garrity. We're paying you time and a half to sit there and freeze your ass off. Stop being a *wuss*."

"What the hell good is time and a half if I freeze to death up here? I felt snow flurries earlier."

"Snow's invigorating," Jack said, as he clicked off his cell phone. He turned to his partner. "Mark, look alive here," he said, snapping his fingers. "That was Garrity. He said everyone's gone from the Rutledge estate. I'm going out there. Kathryn Lucas, the dog, and, from the description Garrity

63

gave me, Myra, too, just left in the rig. I want to know where she's going. Tap into the dispatcher that Lucas works for and get back to me. And keep the tail on the architect. If it looks like she's heading back to the farm, create a diversion so she stays put. And see if you can find a replacement for Garrity. He's getting cranky. If you have to, promise double time. I need someone out there until I do my search."

Mark took off his glasses and started to polish them. "This is not a good thing, Jack. That guy Martin probably has the place rigged with alarms. If you set them off, your ass is grass. We don't have enough money for bail. All right, all right, I'm on it. Be sure you call me every hour on the hour. Just out of curiosity, how do you plan on getting in there?"

Jack smacked at his forehead. "I thought you knew, in my other life I was an electrician. I'm going to short-circuit those gates and walk through or climb over."

Mark groaned and put his glasses back on. He looked like an intelligent owl as he bent down to start hitting the keyboard. He didn't look up when the door slammed behind Jack.

Jack's heart thundered in his chest as he

climbed behind the wheel of his car. He was tingling from head to toe. He could almost smell victory. Halfway to the Rutledge estate he slowed down as a thought hit him. What if it was all a set-up? To his knowledge, Pinewood was never left unattended. Why now? Why would a lady like Myra Rutledge suddenly decide to go for a ride in an eighteen-wheeler? Where did Nikki, the black girl, the Asian girl and Charles Martin go in the Gulfstream? Maybe he shouldn't be so damn hasty. But there was no need to get his ass in a sling. Would he ever get a chance like this again? Probably not.

Jack hit the speed dial on his cell phone. Mark growled a greeting. "It's me, Mark. You get anything on the Gulfstream? They had to file a flight plan. What's taking so long?"

"Shut the hell up, Jack. What's taking so long is I'm trying to access records that aren't supposed to be accessed by the likes of me. From what I can gather, they went to China. That can't be right, can it?"

"You mean the country of China?" *Shit, how brilliant was that?* "Or are you talking about Chinatown in San Francisco or New York?"

"Asia, Jack, Asia. Hong Kong to be

precise. I'm working on it, OK? Where are you?"

Hong Kong! What the hell? Son of a fucking bitch! Jack felt so light-headed he pulled to the side of the country road and rolled down the window. "I'm five minutes from Pinewood," he managed to gasp before he clicked off the cell phone. He took in great gulps of the frigid November air. When he had his wits about him, he leaned back and closed his eyes as his thoughts ran in all directions.

China. Hong Kong. Home of John Chai, the diplomat's son who had killed Myra Rutledge's daughter, Barbara. Coincidence? Unlikely. Three of the women, plus Charles, had gone to China. Two of the women, plus Myra, stayed behind and were now on their way to wherever. Dr. Julia Webster was missing. Maybe she was in China, too. And where the hell was Senator Webster? And Marie Lewellen and her family? Shit! He picked up his cell phone and hit the number one on his speed dial.

"Don't say anything, Mark. Just listen, OK?" He was like a runaway train as he rattled off his suspicions. When he was finished he heard Mark whistle so loud he had to move the phone from his ear.

"They knew Chai would never come

back to the States, so they went there. They're going to kill him, Mark."

"Wait a minute. Just hold on, Jack. If that's true, why didn't Mrs. Rutledge go with them? I'd think she'd want to be part of it. I know I would if it was my kid. Nah, I think you're off base. By the way, the Lucas woman is on her way to Oregon to pick up twenty thousand Christmas trees. She'll drop them off on her way back up the Eastern Seaboard. They're due back in McLean in . . . Who the hell knows? Depends on how fast she drives, I guess. Think about it, Jack. Myra Rutledge is helping Lucas with Christmas trees while her friends go to China to do in her daughter's killer? It's too big a stretch. Fall back and regroup, buddy. Where are you now?"

"Outside the gates of Pinewood. I'm about ready to fry these gates. I'm not wrong, Mark. Don't think for one minute that they didn't get rid of Senator Webster, either. And Marie Lewellen. Now that we know how powerful Charles Martin is, it all makes sense. Factor in Myra Rutledge's money, Nikki's legal expertise and all those other women who probably have special . . . talents, and I make my case."

Jack had to strain to hear Mark's whispered response. "Vigilantes!"

"Yeah. Vigilantes. I'll get back to you. Gotta get to work."

Jack climbed out of his car and looked at the high-tech panel that controlled the gates. A few years ago they were simple gates with a simple code: 1-2-3-4. Nikki had a remote on the visor of her car that she hit and the gates swung open. Mere visitors had to press in the proper code. Less than two years ago these new gates, the kind they had in prisons, were installed with a monitor and a different set of codes. The gates also sounded prison-like, clanging so loudly you had to hold your ears. There was no code these days. The gates were controlled either by someone inside the house or by a special remote control. Why was that?

Jack walked around the back of his car, popped the trunk and took out his brand new Private Dick kit that Mark had assembled for him. He wished now that he had paid more attention to the instructions on all the high-tech gizmos. He knew, though, that Mark had included the instructions. They were probably somewhere in the bottom of the voluminous canvas bag. He dropped the black bag outside the gates and climbed back into the car. He backed it down the road and then drove it into a dense area of wild-looking straggly brush. He looked around for a pine tree, found some saplings, broke off the branches and covered his car. He took a minute to survey the surroundings in case he had to make a hasty retreat. When he had the site firmly locked in his mind he jogged back up the driveway to where his black bag awaited him.

Jack fished around inside the bag until he found the gray box he was looking for. He wished suddenly that he *had* been an electrician in his other life. He carried the box over to the control panel, opened it, looked at the wires and closed his eyes. Red wires, blue wires, yellow wires. Yeah, well, color was color. He hooked on the gray box, hit the plunger and watched the gates give off a shower of sparks. Then he slipped his arms through the straps of the backpack and marched over to the gates, calmly pushed them open, and walked through like he was a regular visitor.

His cell phone chirped. Garrity.

"Gotcha in my sights, Jack. Nice fireworks display. What do you want me to do?"

"Mark is sending a replacement. Stay there till he arrives. Then meet me in the barn. You can hop the fence behind it. We have time before the dogs get here."

"OK. Be careful, Jack. This whole place spooks me big time."

"Keep me in your sights, Garrity. I'm almost to the barn. Call me every ten minutes until your replacement shows up. If you see anyone hovering around, beat feet. Don't join me. You got that?"

"Yeah, Jack. I got it."

Jack stared at the new doors on the barn. Everything around here was new. His mind told him it was probably a set-up, but he was going through with his plan anyway. Maybe a bunch of guys with the special shields were waiting for him in the barn. Maybe this time they'd kill him. Maybe a lot of things.

Jack slipped his arms out of the backpack and rooted around until he found a black box that was guaranteed to give him the right numerical code to any lock. He spent five full minutes reading the instructions before he pressed a series of numbers. He watched the keypad blink as numbers danced across the green bar at the top of the keypad. He heard a click and then the keypad went dark.

"Open Sesame!" Jack chortled. He picked up his backpack and opened the door. All he could see was blackness.

He almost jumped out of his skin when he felt a hand on his shoulder.

"Quick Draw McGraw, you ain't, Jack. I could have plugged you and you never would have known what hit you," Garrity said.

It was true and Jack knew it. "Close the damn door and get in here. We have work to do."

"You have work to do, Jack. I'm outta here. Your guy is up in the tree and has a bead on what's going on. He's got you covered. Call me, but not for twenty-four hours. Good luck, Jack."

Jack nodded. His gut told him he was going to need more than a little good luck. He waited for Garrity to leave before he turned on his high-beam flashlight. He looked around, daunted at what he was seeing. Every inch of floor space was covered with *something.* It would take him days to move things, even if there was room to move the things to.

"Shit!" he muttered.

Five

Li explained that the evening's festivities were being held at a center named Half Moon, Hong Kong's knock-off version of the Taihedian, otherwise known as the Hall of Supreme Harmony, in Beijing. Any event of any importance was held at Half Moon.

"I am very familiar with the entire building, having been there many times. I am also aware of the security measures that go into effect for each and every event, depending of course on the importance of the event and the people involved."

The picture Charles held up was of John Chai at his Harvard graduation. The picture was on the grainy side, and Chai looked extremely young. Li had supplied an updated picture taken a year ago on May Day. Chai was not a tall man and Li commented that he suffered from a Napoleon complex. Rumors abounded that Chai liked long-legged, blond American women. It was also rumored that he was not a kind, gentle lover.

"He has a mean streak in him and no one ever says no to John Chai. Especially women. As you all know, women are second-class citizens in China."

"Does he work?" Alexis asked.

Li cleared his throat. "I believe he makes an appearance from time to time at his family's export business. He is what you Americans call a playboy. It is said he is heavy-handed with everyone he comes in contact with, especially women. He works very hard at perfecting his image. He wants to be a tough guy like the American gangsters in your films."

"He likes to play, does he? So do we. How exciting," Nikki said flatly.

Li raised his white head to look into Nikki's eyes. He turned away quickly to stare at his old friend Charles. Charles gave an elaborate shrug as if to say *What did you expect?*

Charles looked down at the Rolex on his wrist. "We should be going, Li. I don't think it wise to arrive fashionably late so as to draw attention to ourselves." He looked around at the three women and nodded. "You look stunning, all three of you. One last word of caution: sip your drinks. You're going to need your wits about you."

The women watched as the two old friends walked away. They followed at a discreet distance so as not to hear their conversation.

"Anyone nervous?" Nikki asked.

"I feel like a cat on a hot griddle," Alexis said.

"I am worried. Stay close to me so I can interpret for you. Watch what I do and do the same thing. I am not experienced in this culture even though I speak the language. I have never set foot in this country before. I was born in the United States. But I will do my best," Yoko muttered.

"That's good enough for us," Nikki said. "We all agreed that the three of us will give Chai the come-on and then back off. We're going to make him chase us. He's not used to that, so we're going to make him work for the privilege of our company. Is it true, Yoko, that Chinese men have little . . . ?"

Yoko flushed a rosy pink. "The aunts who raised me say it is so."

"Uh-huh," Alexis said with a straight face. "A Napoleon complex *and* a shortage where it counts the most."

Nikki laughed, an evil sound.

"Ladies, our car is here. Careful now,"

Charles said as he held the door open for them to slide into the back. He then took his seat next to Li in the second section of the limousine. Jay was their chauffeur for the evening.

"What will we do if the weasel doesn't fall for our assorted charms?" Alexis asked.

"I'm not sure, but I think the possibility of a *ménage* . . . whatever will pique his interest. Practice your come-hither looks, ladies, and be prepared to beat Mr. Chai off with a stick."

Nikki laughed again. "Take a good look at us, Alexis. How could Chai not be attracted to us? We're stunning. We sizzle and we look sensual. It's all in the eyes. Remember that. I am not worried about him being attracted to us at all. We all rehearsed our Washington and Boston small talk and we have it down pat. He's going to want to show off for us. All we have to do is act like he isn't impressing us and then home in on someone less attractive than him — and someone who is *taller*. That alone will make him nuts. Little guys hate big guys."

"I have a question," Yoko said. "What if . . . what if Chai's people go after Mr. Li once we are gone? He is a frail old man and should be able to live out his years in peace and harmony."

Nikki nodded as she stared out the limo window into the surrounding darkness. "I worry about that, too. I can't be sure about this, but I think Charles will offer to take him with us. Charles told me earlier that Mr. Li's office is one of those rooms covert operatives use that can be *vaporized* when the room is no longer functional. Super-spy stuff. I sensed that Mr. Li is a man at peace with everything in his life. He's helping us willingly. I don't know what will happen to him. I would hate to take away the thought that he might be sent to the Su-Chou prison for helping us. I personally would feel better if he leaves with us. But in the end, it will be up to Mr. Li."

"Perhaps it is a mistake to invite Mr. Chai back here to Mr. Li's house," Alexis said.

"I don't think we have any other choice, Alexis. Besides, Mr. Li's airstrip is close by. We'll get out of here as quickly as possible. Oh, we're slowing down. Wow! The young lady who's getting engaged must be very popular. Look at all those people going into the building."

"Never mind the people, Nikki. Look at

the building!" Alexis said, awe ringing in her voice.

The women stopped to admire the Half Moon building. Never having seen the real Hall of Supreme Harmony, they could only marvel at the thousands of tiny lights that lit up the three-tier marble terrace leading to the main building.

Charles turned around and hissed. "Later you can admire it on the Internet. Look alive, ladies."

"Oh, poop," Alexis muttered. "We should be admiring it now, in person. Would you look at those bronze dings. Bet neither of you know they're a kind of Chinese vessel representing the eighteen national provinces of the times. Look up there at that luxurious balustraded terrace and you can see a bronze crane and a bronze tortoise, both symbols of everlasting rule and longevity."

"And you know all this . . . how?" Nikki asked, craning her neck to see the crane and the tortoise.

"I read the papers Charles gave us. For a knockoff, it's rather grand. Can you picture yourself getting married in a place like this? Think of how many people you could invite and how many presents you'd get from those people."

"No more chatter, ladies. We're about to enter the great hall. Be demure. Do not overstate your Americanism. And remember, sip your drinks."

Alexis looked from Nikki to Yoko and then down at her shimmering gown. "I can't believe he dressed us like this and now he wants demure. OK, demure it is."

"Come, ladies, it's time to meet the groom's family," Li said quietly. "They are kind people. Unassuming and incredibly rich."

Ninety minutes into the party Nikki realized she was bored. She hated flute music. As far as she could see there wasn't one unattached handsome man to be seen. All the women appeared to have escorts except for Alexis, Yoko, and herself. And no man was paying any attention to them.

"Let's check out the dining table. I don't see *him* anywhere, do you?"

Nikki moved off in the direction of the buffet table, Alexis and Yoko in her wake. Eyes turned to follow the three unattached women. They heard whispers as they passed by.

"They must be American . . . Their posture screams America . . . The gowns are exquisite, must be American designers. Beautiful," followed them.

Nikki looked at the array of food. "This is . . . ?"

"Octopus," Yoko volunteered. "And eel, and a few other things you won't care for. We can pretend we're dieting and eat the snow peas and some rice. Or we can go straight to the dessert table and choose a rice cake."

Nikki turned around to respond to Yoko, but her gaze was everywhere. "He should be here by now. If he's a no-show, we're in trouble."

"He will be here, Nikki. His father would insist. Possibly later. As you can see, these affairs are on the boring side. Being here, displaying one's family as a unit, is what is important. For Mr. Chai not to appear would be to dishonor his own family. Please, people are watching us. Choose some food and move to the end of the table. And keep smiling," Yoko said.

Nikki did as instructed and moved off. Suddenly she felt a hand on her arm. She turned to see Li escorting the prospective bride and groom to her side. He made the introductions. Everyone smiled. Everyone bowed.

To Nikki's unpracticed eye, the young couple looked like a couple of kids playing

79

grown-up, but Li had said they were both twenty-three.

Yet Kwai, the bride, suddenly grinned and said, "So, how do you like this shindig? On a scale of one to ten I'd personally give it a one. However, one must do what family wants in my country. When Jin and I return to California our friends plan to throw a real party for us. Dancing, beer, wine, chips and salsa and some real rock music." She giggled and the others smiled. Suddenly remembering her manners, Yet Kwai — who said her name meant beautiful rose — said, "I love your gowns. I love everything American, but don't tell that to my parents."

She was an imp, and Nikki warmed to the young woman right away. "I understand you attend Stanford and Jin attends Berkeley. Do you plan on staying in America or will you return to your homeland?"

"We'll stay for a few years but then we will return. It is expected. Over the Christmas holidays we're going to a dude ranch in Nevada." Peals of laughter from Yet Kwai. "Jin wants to see what it's like to be a cowboy. During spring break we're both doing Outward Bound. It's a test of endurance and survival. I am honored to have met you, but now I must circulate. Enjoy yourselves as much as you can at this stuffy party," she giggled before she moved off.

The three women moved off with their gold-encrusted plates that held nothing more than a tablespoon of rice and snow peas.

"I think I'd kill for a Big Mac right now," Alexis mumbled.

"Yet Kwai is right, this is the stuffiest party I've ever been to," Nikki said. "All those fire-eating dragons attached to the wall are so . . . boring. Have you ever seen so many urns and five-foot-tall vases in your life? I wonder what time it is."

"I think this stuffy party is about due to liven up. Charles and Mr. Li are bringing John Chai to us. He looks *slick*. I say we show some bad American manners and cut him down to size immediately," Alexis said.

Nikki's lips barely moved when she responded. "I can do that with no problem. Back me up and follow my lead. Pretend we don't see them and move off to the left."

"Miss Quinn, one moment," Li said as he realized their intent and quickened his stride.

Nikki stopped, turned and looked up at the tall Chinese man. "Yes, Mr. Li?"

"I would like to introduce you three lovely ladies to Mr. John Chai. John lived in America for quite a few years. I thought you might like to chat about your country."

Nikki looked at the man standing in front of her. Barbara's killer. She had to fight with herself to remain calm. What she wanted to do was rip out his tongue, gouge out his eyes, disembowel him and then slice off his ugly head. If she did all those things she wondered how long it would take for him to bleed out. A minute, she decided.

"Not really," she drawled.

John Chai raised one eyebrow and stared into Nikki's eyes.

He was a predator, pure and simple. Well, she'd had dealings with predators before. Nikki shrugged and took a step to the left. "It was nice meeting you, Mr. Chai. Come along, girls, there must be some tall men around here somewhere. Otherwise, we're outta here."

John Chai looked stunned. Mr. Li smirked and moved off quickly.

"Wait, please," Chai managed to say as he reached for Nikki's arm.

Nikki looked pointedly at the man's

hand on her arm. She shook it off. "Don't ever touch my person, Mr. Chai, or you'll find yourself in one of those dragon's mouths. You're insulting me. Imagine what a commotion that would cause at this stuffy little get-together."

"My apologies, Miss Quinn. Can we please start over? I take responsibility for my bad manners. It won't happen again." He turned to Alexis. "Has anyone ever told you that you look like Halle Berry?"

Alexis smirked. "No. But people have told me Halle Berry looks like me. The truth is, I'm better-looking and I have longer legs."

Taken aback, Chai was at a loss for words. He tried again and looked at Yoko who stared at him with revulsion. "Where were you born?"

"Why do you want to know? Are you writing a book?"

Chai threw his hands in the air as if to say, *You Americans!* "I was trying to make party conversation. These affairs are incredibly boring, as you can see. I thought since you came unescorted, as I did, that perhaps we could hang out together to get through the evening."

"I find you as boring as this party, Mr. Chai. You people don't know what a party is. What do you suppose would happen if I climbed up on one of those tables and started to sing and dance?" Nikki looked him up and down, stopping at his waist. She gave him a twisted grin before she stepped away. John Chai was left standing alone, his mouth wide open.

Alexis said, just loud enough for Chai to hear, "I sure hope Mr. Li can find some interesting men to join us at his home after the party. I'd hate to think I wasted two thousand dollars on a dress just for this affair."

"I think I need some air," Nikki said.

Outside on one of the wide marble terraces, Nikki leaned over and pretended to retch. "Do you have any idea how hard that was? I'm sorry, of course you do. The man is a pus ball. He's greasy, oily, unctuous and his eyes are dead. Did you see the way he undressed us all with those eyes? I wanted to kill him. Did he hear what you said, Alexis?"

"I think I said it loud enough. Mr. Li will make the arrangements if he doesn't ask to be invited back to his house. Don't look now, but here comes the little shit again."

Nikki whirled around.

"I hope I'm not intruding, ladies. I came

to apologize for what I'm assuming is bad behavior on my part. Please, let me make it up to you."

Nikki rolled her eyes as though nothing he could say or do would interest her.

"And how would you go about doing that, Mr. Chai?" Yoko queried.

"By showing you the nightlife in Hong Kong. It's very interesting and exciting."

"Some other time," Nikki said. "I doubt your nightlife can compare to nightlife in America. Now, should you ever find yourself in our neck of the woods, we could really show you what a party is."

"Do you ever go to the States, Mr. Chai?" Yoko asked.

"Call me John. No, I don't go to the States. My home is here. However, I was educated at Harvard."

"Big deal. Half the world went to Harvard. Now, if you told me you were some high-ranking government official or a diplomat, that would impress me. I graduated from Yale. We Yalies have no respect for you Harvard guys. Wimps. Wusses," Nikki said. "Lace on your underwear."

John Chai's voice took on an edge that hadn't been there previously. "Is there a reason you're being so rude to me when I'm trying to be nice to you?"

Nikki looked him up and down again. "You don't interest me."

Chai laughed but it was an embarrassed sound. "What would make me interesting to you, Miss Quinn?"

Nikki hoped what she was feeling didn't show on her face. "Perhaps knowing you had a sense of adventure. That you liked to skirt danger. I'm not interested in fly-fishing, smoking pot and drinking myself silly so that I don't remember what happened the next day. I like a man who is devilishly clever, experimental and who thinks for himself. Again, it was nice meeting you, Mr. Chai." Then she said to the others, "We must be off, girls. I'm sure Mr. Li is ready to leave and we certainly don't want to keep him waiting, now do we?"

There was nothing for John Chai to do but move aside and allow the three women to walk past him. Alexis winked and pinched his cheek. "I bet we could have had a swell time. Ah, well, if you ever come to the States, look us up. We're in the phone book."

Nikki looked toward the carved double doors that stood open. The families of Yet Kwai and Jin stood at the entrance. More bowing was going on. The line was endless as far as one could see. Where was Li? More important, where was Charles? She'd barely seen him all evening.

"There must be another exit, girls. I'm not up to standing in that line in these shoes. We'll be here till midnight."

"Allow me to escort you ladies to your car," Chai said gallantly. "There is an exit off the terrace. I must warn you that you will be accused of having bad American manners if you choose to use that particular exit. By the way, Mr. Li has kindly extended an invitation to my family to attend the little two-day gathering at his home. Unfortunately, my father has other pressing matters to take care of, so I will be attending in his place. I look forward to getting to know you ladies better."

"Ask me if I care," Alexis snapped. "Lead the way, Mr. Chai."

"How nice," Nikki mumbled. *Where was Charles?* "Won't that interfere with all the security you people have surrounding you? There's nothing worse than security spying on your every move."

"We are going to the country where Mr. Li resides. There is no need for security. I, too, hate to have people watching my every move. Ah, now we are clear of the crowds. Tell me, which is Mr. Li's car?"

"Now, how would we know that?" Yoko snarled. "All the vehicles look alike."

Nikki tried to squelch the panic that was threatening to engulf her. Where was Charles? For that matter, where was Li? She could feel the weasel behind her breathing on her neck. And then she saw both men. Charles had his cell phone to his ear and Mr. Li was smoking a cigar. They were walking toward them. "Thank you, God. Thank you, God," she said silently.

Six

Jack looked around the crowded barn. "Son of a bitch!" he snarled when he saw a rat scurrying past him. In all his life he'd never seen such a pile of junk. Why would Myra save the ancient Duesenberg with the four flat tires? To cover the floor, of course. Obviously the car wasn't going anywhere. Neither was the wagon that was loaded with hundred-pound bags of rock salt. The bags were stacked up under the wagon, too. He estimated two hundred bags in total. He could try to move the bags, but where the hell would he move them to? He shone the flashlight on a tractor lawnmower that was just as rusted as the Duesenberg.

Jack debated calling Conway, Garrity's replacement, but nixed the idea almost immediately. If there was a secret trapdoor in this barn it was going to stay a secret unless he had a warrant to move everything out. He'd need a crew of at least ten men to clear this junk pile.

His options had just run out when his cell phone chirped. He growled a greeting. "I'm in the barn, Mark, and there's no way in hell I can move any of this crap. I'm going to give the house a shot."

"Jack, don't even think about breaking into the house. You've been lucky so far. I told you, we don't have enough money in the bank to post bail for you."

"Listen to me, Mark. When am I ever going to get another chance at this place? It's like goddamn Fort Knox. If that gizmo you gave me opened the gate, why won't it give me the code for the inside alarm system?"

"I don't know that it will and I don't know that it won't. At best you would probably have forty-five seconds to get in and disarm the system. If you aren't successful, all the bells and whistles will go off and they will rupture your eardrums. You willing to take that chance?"

"Hell, yes. If that happens, I can be out of here in five seconds and over the fence to the forest. I hid my car. It will take the cops at least ten minutes to get here, maybe longer. C'mon, buddy, show me some support here."

"Jack . . . OK, OK, but leave the line open. Where are you now?"

"I'm on the back stoop where the kitchen door is. I can see the alarm from where I'm standing. I can pick this lock with no problem. OK, I got it open. The alarm is beeping."

"You ass, turn on the gray box."

Jack did and waited. He had a feeling he knew the code, Barbara's birth date. He wasn't surprised when the numbers flashed green on the gray box. Jack pressed in the numbers and the high-pitched beeping stopped. He was in and he was safe. "I'll call you back, Mark. Oh, wait, what's the story on the architect?"

"My guy disabled her car. That's not to say she won't rent another one, but for now you're safe. Conway is up in the tree and has his eye on you. Don't forget the dogs arrive at five. You have to turn the power to the gates back on before the guy gets there."

"Yeah, yeah, yeah," Jack said, clicking off the phone. He looked down at his watch. Hell, he had *hours*.

Jack made himself at home by making a pot of coffee. While he waited for the water to drip through the filter, he picked ham off a bone that was in the refrigerator. All the while his brain raced. There would be no way to the tunnels from the second

91

floor, so he had to concentrate on the first floor. He'd start with the basement. He tried to remember what Nikki had told him about the tunnels. She'd never said anything about a secret opening. She'd also never said how she and Barbara got to the tunnels. Through the basement? How else?

Jack poured black coffee into an oversize mug and carried it with him when he opened the cellar door. He turned on the light switch and made his way cautiously down the steep flight of narrow steps. He walked around, trying to figure out where a trapdoor could possibly be located. If one of the tunnels led to the barn, the opening should be right about where he was standing. The only problem was, he was standing on a concrete floor that had no cracks and nothing that could pass for a trapdoor.

Jack picked up a broom handle and started tapping the wooden walls. They all gave off the same sound. No false doors. He focused on the shelves, where he could see jars of home-canned peaches. Maybe there was an opening behind the shelves. He gave up that idea when he saw the thick cobwebs and dirt. Everything in this basement had layers and layers of dust.

It was like any other basement, full of junk and odds and ends. Still, he wasn't giving up. He continued to poke and shove. He moved an ancient ice box — nothing. Maybe Myra was a pack rat and couldn't bear to part with her junk. It was unlikely that any of the clutter was being kept for sentimental reasons.

An hour later, Jack stomped his way back upstairs to the kitchen. He didn't bother to look back. If he had, he would have seen the footprints he left behind. He closed and locked the cellar door before he poured himself a second cup of coffee, then called Mark to report his lack of progress.

"Check out Charles Martin's room, Jack. Listen, I really don't know much about old slave houses and the like, but doesn't it stand to reason they wouldn't have an opening in the basement? Wouldn't that be the first place one would look? I'm thinking it's probably some kind of secret opening. Try tapping the walls. That's what they do in the movies."

"This isn't a movie, Mark. I'm watching the time. I'll call you back."

This time Jack left his coffee on the table. He galloped up the staircase to the second floor. He'd been here before but for some reason the house now looked more lived in. He smelled perfume as he walked from one room to another. He looked through everything, trying to figure out who slept where. He knew where Nikki's room was. She'd shared it with Barbara when they were kids. She still slept here from the looks of things. He moved around but didn't touch anything. He opened a closet and saw many garments he recognized. Nikki must be using a new perfume these days. He closed his eyes and let his senses and his memory go astray. He forced himself to move out of the room. His eyes burned unbearably. Must have been all that dust in the cellar.

Myra and Charles's room. So neat and tidy. King-size bed. Triple dresser, double walk-in closet. Two bathrooms. His and hers. Well, why the hell not? When you had money you could have two bathrooms back to back. The bathrooms here were bigger than his bedroom in the apartment he shared with Mark.

Everything was luxurious, the carpeting lush and ankle deep. The draperies were a rich champagne color and were drawn across the windows. A fire was laid in the huge fireplace. Two deep matching recliners sat next to the fireplace with small folding trays beside them. The old folks probably ate breakfast or had late-night snacks while they watched the news. On the opposite wall a giant television screen waited to be turned on. A person could literally live in this room.

Jack moved to the dressing room, which was lined with mirrors. Nothing there. He looked behind the pictures hanging on the walls. No wall safe anywhere. Nothing in the bathroom or the linen closet. He moved over to Charles's closet. Clothes, shoes, winter wear, summer wear, luggage. Nothing personal. Not even a check book or a receipt of any kind. He pawed through the dresser drawers. Underwear, socks, tee shirts, pajamas. Nothing underneath. No false bottoms to the drawers. Zip. His shoulders sagged as he went through Myra's things, knowing full well that he wasn't going to find anything.

Back on the first floor, he called Mark again to report on his lack of success. He expected some kind of harangue and was surprised to hear him say, "Think about it, Jack. Don't you find that weird? Where is his personal stuff? Put yourself in his place. Where would you stash your past life? It's a given that you wouldn't totally discard it. I suppose he might keep things in a safe deposit box, but for some reason I don't think so. A man like him, with his past, he'd want to keep it close to his chest. My advice is to keep looking and watch the time. Is there an office anywhere in the house?"

"No, but there's a library. No desk, though. Which makes me wonder where they sit down to pay their bills."

"They probably do it electronically. Keep looking, Jack. 'Bye."

Jack prowled and paced, banging walls, kicking furniture, and cursing. He dropped to his knees and crawled around the rooms to check the baseboards, lifted area carpets looking for a trapdoor. He went to the kitchen to look through the drawers in the hope of finding a magnifying glass. He found a small one and was again on his knees inspecting the rosettes on the carved mantel when his cell phone chirped. He clicked it on as he pressed the magnifying glass to his eye. He saw the button at the same instant that Conway barked, "Get your ass outta there, Jack. Company. The man with the dogs. You got two minutes to get that fence back on and outta there. Go, Jack!"

"Son of a bitch!" Jack raced through the house, set the alarm in the kitchen, barreled through the door and out to the gates where he held up the gray box. He watched as the gates sizzled to life. In the time it took his heart to beat five times, he raced across the driveway and threw himself over the chain-link fence. Disoriented by his fall, he staggered off. He had no idea where he was in relation to Conway until he heard him.

"Over here, drop down, Jack," Conway hissed. Jack dropped and crawled through the brush.

"Those dogs have your scent, Jack. Jesus, will you listen to them? Shit, man, they're up on the stoop and the trainer is looking around. They know. Come on, Jack, we need to haul ass."

They were clear of the property in less than eight minutes. "I gotta get my car outta there. Check out that guy, can you see anything with those binoculars?"

"No, too much brush. Don't even think about asking me to climb another tree. We have to get out of here."

"I can't leave my car there. I want to wait till the trainer leaves. I don't think he called the police. He's probably checking everything outside. For all he knows a stray cat or even a fox could have gotten in. He's not going to want to make waves with the cops over something like that. Shhh, I hear a car engine."

A black Lincoln Navigator crawled down the driveway, the driver scanning both sides of the road. In the dense underbrush, Jack's heart pumped furiously. His sigh of relief when the Navigator passed was so loud that Conway clamped his hand over Jack's mouth.

Within minutes, Jack had the evergreens thrown aside and was behind the wheel. He backed out to the gravel road and then got out of the car. He looked down at his license plate, gave a mighty tug, and the screws came loose. He threw the plate in the back seat and barreled down the road.

He saw the Navigator just as the driver spotted him. Jack backed up, thanking God they were the only two vehicles on the road, and stormed away in the opposite direction. The Navigator gave chase but Jack had taken more than one defensive driving course during his stint with the prosecutor's office. He lost the huge SUV within ten miles by peeling off and going down secondary roads to meet roads that were little more than paths. He was back out on the highway, headed in the opposite direction, before the guy in the Navigator knew what had happened.

When he finally made it to the store-front office, Jack collapsed into his swivel chair. "Get me something to calm me down. I don't even care if it's Valium. You aren't going to fucking believe what I have to tell you, Mark."

Mark handed Jack a frosty bottle of Michelob. "Jack, I believe everything you tell me no matter how unbelievable it sounds. What the hell happened?"

Jack told him. "I have to go back, but I can't do it till morning when that guy picks up the dogs. My biggest worry is did he call the cops. I'm inclined to think he didn't. He did give chase but he didn't see me. I gotta tell you, Mark, something made me rip off that license plate. Talk about gut feelings and sixth senses. I'd be behind bars right now if I hadn't done that. The bastard was just out there on the side of the road, *waiting*."

The only thing Mark heard were the words I have to go back.

"Don't you think that guy or the cops will be out there tomorrow morning? How do you think you're going to get in and out again?"

Jack's fingers raked his hair. "Not the way I got in today, that's for sure. I'll go in the way Conway goes in and jump the

99

fence back by the barn where the ground dips. I can do it, Mark, so get that look off your face. I'm doing it. I found it! I know that button on the carving is the way they go in and out. I saw it through the magnifying glass. I'm not wrong. I was *that* close and then had to split. *That* close, Mark. Damn, I'd go back there right now if those damn dogs weren't there."

"That's definitely not an option at the moment. Let me read up on those directions again. Maybe I can turn off the gates from Conway's spot or by coming up toward the house from the other side. Maybe there's a way to modify the gray box. I'm going with you and I think we should take Conway with us. By the way, where is he?"

"I sent him home. He's spooked. Besides, even with all his body warmers, it's forty-four degrees outside. Give him a call and tell him to meet us out there at seven."

"What if the architect shows up?"

"Call the guys to make sure that doesn't happen. All we need is an hour in that house, Mark. We're going to need a good camera."

Mark groaned as he opened a second bottle of beer for Jack and one for himself.

Jack held his bottle aloft. "Here's to the word surprise!"

"Bull*shit!* Here's to a prison cell and no bail!"

"I'm not drinking to that!"

Mark started to laugh and couldn't stop. "Then you're a bigger asshole than I thought you were." Before they knew what was happening they were both rolling on the floor, pummeling one another, laughing their heads off.

Seven

Kathryn Lucas sat across the table from Myra, her thoughts running in all directions as she watched Myra gobble down what Kathryn called truckers' home-cooked food.

"This is so wonderful, so tasty. I don't think I've ever eaten so much grease at one sitting. I can't wait to tell Charles."

Kathryn grinned. "Are you going to tell him you heard your arteries snap shut?"

"I think I'll leave that part out. I am so glad you invited me along. I haven't done anything this exciting in twenty years. Charles is never going to believe I went on this little road trip. You don't happen to have a camera, do you, dear?"

"Nope, but we can buy a throwaway one at the register when we pay our bill. Posterity, huh? I'm so glad you're enjoying the thrill of the open road."

"What I like is the camaraderie. You seem to know everyone. Are your colleagues always this friendly?"

"Yes, and every single one of them would drop what they're doing to help another trucker. Remember how they blocked the highway that time Jack Emery sent out an APB on me? Believe it or not, Myra, the truckers could bring the country to a standstill if they wanted to. They're good, hard-working people trying to earn a living to support their families. It's not an easy life, nor is it a glamorous one. Did you have fun talking to them on the horn?"

"Absolutely. I wish I could meet them in person sometime. Do you think they'd remember me?"

"Hey, if you want an invitation to the Truckers' Ball, I can arrange it. It's always held in the spring."

"I would love to attend. I'll send back my RSVP the minute I get the invitation."

Kathryn laughed. "It doesn't work that way. We just get on the horn, pass the word and everyone shows up at a designated truck stop. Each year it's held at a different place."

"Be sure to count me in as a yes. Can I bring Charles?"

"Absolutely. Speaking of Charles, shouldn't he have called us by now?"

Myra tipped her Redskins cap further back on her springy curls. "I was thinking the same thing. I'm sure he's calling the house and leaving messages. Maybe his cell phone doesn't work in China."

"Well, hi there, gorgeous!" a jolly voice said.

Myra and Kathryn both looked up to see a giant of a man towering over them. Murphy was licking at his hand. Myra assumed the comment was made to Kathryn and said, "She is beyond gorgeous."

"Not her! She's too young and skinny for my taste. 'Sides, she's young enough to be my granddaughter and this dog of hers is a killer, as you can see. I was talking to you, honey."

Myra was so flustered she knocked her glass of water over. In her haste to mop up the spill with paper napkins she sent her breakfast plate flying off the table. The giant caught it with one hand that was as big as a ham hock.

"How about having a cup of joe with me, sweet cheeks?"

"Why I . . . That is so . . . Do you really think I'm gorgeous?" Myra asked boldly, her cheeks flaming pink. *Sweet cheeks!* She realized suddenly that the giant was staring at her sweatshirt. She tried to hunch her shoulders so he couldn't read the words.

"Takes a lot to earn a shirt like that. Introduce me to your partner, Sis."

"Was wondering when you were going to get around to that. Stop being so nice to my dog. I saw that bacon you slipped him. Merry Widow, meet Big Bear. Bear, meet the gorgeous Widow."

The giant reached for Myra's hand and brought it to his lips. "This day will stay in my mind forever." Murphy howled so loud the other diners stopped eating to see what the commotion was all about.

"The pleasure . . . the pleasure is all mine, Bear." Myra gulped. *Oh God, Charles, you are never going to believe this!*

"Where you headed, Bear?" Kathryn asked.

"I'm off for thirty-six. Just unloaded kitchen appliances at Home Depot. I go north to the mountains at the end of the thirty-six, how about you?"

"I'm picking up twenty thousand Christmas trees that go up the Eastern Seaboard, then home till after the holidays. See ya next year."

But Bear wasn't finished yet. He eyed Myra and bent over to whisper something in her ear. Myra smiled. "I'll be sure to save a spot on my dance card for you . . .

ah . . . Bear." Murphy howled again. This time the customers ignored his outrage.

"Time to go, Myra," Kathryn said. She placed a twenty-dollar bill under the salt shaker and said, "These girls work hard for their money. Now, are you sure you don't want to pay the five bucks to take a shower and put on some clean duds?"

"No, dear, I'm fine." Myra looked around the busy truck stop. Steam billowed up from the grill as waitresses and cooks shouted to one another. The truckers joined in, adding quick fixes for certain recipes. It was a friendly atmosphere. The red Formica table tops with the cracked leather booths added character to this thriving place on the road to nowhere. Myra enjoyed every minute, especially eating the greasy food that was so delicious, she'd asked for seconds.

As they wound their way through the crowd of truckers Kathryn was stopped a dozen times. Some of the truckers she hugged, some she shook hands with, some she patted on the back. The smile never left her face as she talked and laughed with them. It was easy to see that she was well liked. Myra felt proud to walk alongside her.

They were almost at the door when

Kathryn heard her name called. She turned to see one of the weary waitresses rush up to her. "I didn't know you were here, Kathryn. It's been a madhouse here all day. Listen, yesterday word came down that Curly Cue's wife was in a bad car accident. They're on one of those shitty HMOs and they're going to need some help. We're taking up a collection."

Kathryn and Myra both emptied out their pockets.

"Miss, do you have a pencil?" Myra asked. The waitress looked at her but handed over her pencil and a slip from her order booklet. Myra scribbled Nikki's name, the name of her law firm, and the phone number. "This is my daughter and she distributes money from a defunct HMO. She'll be glad to help you. Call her in two days. I'll talk to her myself when we get home. Tell Curly Cue and his wife not to worry, everything will be taken care of."

The waitress looked over at Kathryn to see if Myra was blowing hot air. Kathryn nodded. "Be sure to do it, Arlene. Tell Curly Cue I said merry Christmas. See ya next time I come this way."

Outside in the frosty Oregon air, Myra took off her baseball cap and slapped it against her leg the way she'd seen the other truckers do. Kathryn giggled all the way to the gas pump where she inserted her credit card to pay for the gas. "Thank God for plastic. Thirty more minutes and we load the trees and head for home. You tired, Myra?"

She was, but she wouldn't admit it for the world. "Not at all, dear. Do you think we should try calling Charles again? And Isabelle. She should have called us. Dear Lord, I hope nothing is wrong."

"Nothing is wrong. Charles allowed for everything and anything. Isabelle, now, that's a different story. Soon as we get out of this zoo and on the road, I'll call her again. I'm sure there are at least a dozen messages on your answering machine at home. Are you sure you can't retrieve the messages by phone?"

"I'm sure. It's just an old-fashioned answering machine that sits next to the phone. Nikki wanted me to get voicemail but you have to remember so many numbers, I decided I didn't need it. Now, of course, I wish I had. I do hope Charles isn't upset. If I had been thinking clearly before we left, I could have put a new message on the machine. Oh, well, there's no point in worrying about it now. That man

Bear called me sweet cheeks. That was so . . . sweet of him. He was flirting with me. At my age. Don't tell Charles, but I loved it. Just loved it."

"I know. You pinked up pretty good back there. Bear is a honey. He loves classical music, goes to the ballet when he can. He has season tickets to the opera but rarely gets to go. And he reads romance novels by the dozen. Actually, he listens to them on tape. He said he's learned more from them than from actual real-life situations. He claims that if the right woman ever falls in his lap he'll know just how to treat her. The funny thing is, he means it. OK, here's the cell phone. Call Isabelle."

Myra pressed in the number and listened to it ringing. "A voice is asking me if I want to leave a message. I'm to press one if I do . . . Isabelle, dear, please call Kathryn as soon as you can. We've been trying to reach you since yesterday. We're on the road, about to pick up the Christmas trees. I'll leave the cell phone on and wait for your call."

"That's not like Isabelle," Kathryn said. "I wonder if . . . Maybe something *is* wrong, Myra. Isabelle is conscientious, so it's not like her not to call. See if you can get her regular home phone number from the information operator. She lives in Arlington."

Myra did as instructed. Then her shoulders slumped. "Isabelle has an unpublished number and they won't give it out. I have her number at home in my Rolodex but that won't do us any good. What should we do, Kathryn?"

"There's nothing we can do, Myra, until we get home or Charles calls us. I have an idea. I can drop you off at the nearest airport and you can fly home. Take a car service from the airport. We both have to get at least three or four hours' sleep. You can be home in that amount of time. That's if you're really worried. If not, we'll continue as we are."

"No, no, Kathryn, I'm staying with you."

"OK then, there's the depot, and they're waiting for us. Wait till we're back on the road to make the call. It won't take long to load the trees. We'll be out of here in about an hour. Stretch your legs while I check the manifest. Stay, Murph," she ordered the German shepherd before she jumped out of the truck to unlock the back. She shoved the door up. "We're going to be smelling balsam all the way home."

Myra trotted around, trying to look like

she knew what she was doing. This was such an adventure and she wanted to savor every minute of it. Until she'd gone on the road with Kathryn she hadn't realized how boring her life was. Even with the Sisterhood, and that her own revenge was finally underway, something was missing. Not that hitting the road in an eighteen-wheeler was the answer, but it did shake away her doldrums.

Myra did her best to stay out of everyone's way. Truckers doffed their caps to her, waved, grinned, asked how it was going, to which she responded the way she thought Kathryn would. "Things are great, nice seeing you, what's up," that kind of thing. She high-tailed it to the side as a rig pulled in, did a quick turn and backed up next to Kathryn's rig. She sniffed the heady scent of the balsam, a smell she loved. She watched for a few minutes as men started loading the trees into the back of the truck. She'd wondered how it was possible to load twenty thousand trees into one huge truck, but now she saw. Twenty trees to a bundle that were wrapped in some kind of wire mesh. Each bundle was tagged with a destination. Big trees were loaded first, then the rest were loaded according to size, right down to the smallest three-footers.

Myra walked around to the side to make sure she was out of the way. She could hear the men barking orders and clearly heard the conversation of the two men assigned to load Kathryn's truck. They were laughing and joking. With nothing else to do, she listened, her eyes popping at what she was hearing. Someone named Duke appeared, his voice a low growl.

"C'mon, c'mon, move it. She's no dummy. You want her climbing up here checking those bundles? C'mon, we got a sweet thing going, eighteen hundred bucks split three ways is Christmas money for the kids. No one is going to miss two trees to a bundle. You need to work faster."

Myra tried to do the math in her head. Four hundred trees. They were stealing four hundred trees from Kathryn. Trees that sold from seventy-five dollars to one hundred and fifty dollars. Would Kathryn have to pay back the money? Would they call her a thief? Every business would be short-changed two trees to a bundle. If Kathryn was signing off on twenty thousand trees, she would be held responsible. Myra ran as fast as her legs would carry her, dodging truckers and rigs, until she found Kathryn. She yanked at her arm and dragged her to the side. Breathless, she blurted what she'd heard.

Kathryn dropped her clipboard to the ground and ran to her truck. A moment later Murphy was at her side and she was carrying a shotgun that she fired in the air. The depot turned silent when Kathryn clicked back the hammer for another shot.

"Don't forget those four hundred trees you're planning on keeping for yourselves! Load them in there now and get the hell away from this truck!"

It took a solid hour to clear it all up, with Kathryn and Myra inside the truck counting trees as other truckers helped load. The police arrived and carted off the three men with apologies from the managers of the depot.

Thirty minutes later, every truck in the depot sounded its horn as Kathryn headed out. She gave her own horn two sharp blasts in return. "Myra, you just earned that shirt you're wearing. It's yours forever and ever."

"And I'll treasure it forever and ever."

Myra soon dozed for a while but woke when the cell phone in her hand buzzed. "Should I answer it or do you want to answer it?"

"This is a tricky road with a lot of

hairpin turns, so I need to pay attention to what I'm doing. You answer it, Myra."

Myra's voice was neutral. "Hello?"

"Myra, is that you? This is Isabelle. I'm trying to reach Kathryn."

"She's right here in the truck with me, dear. Or maybe I'm right here with her. We're together," Myra said firmly. "We've been trying to reach you. Are you at the farm?"

"No, Myra, I'm home. Someone broke into my car and stole everything, even the cell phone Charles gave me. I had it programmed with everyone's number. Whoever broke into my car damaged the transmission. I don't have the money to fix it. I can't rent a car because I don't have credit cards. I'm stuck here. I haven't been able to get to the farm. I have been calling every sequence of numbers I could in the hope of reaching Kathryn. If your next question is have I heard from Charles, the answer is no. That doesn't mean he hasn't called and whoever stole the cell phone answered it. Have you heard from him?"

"No, dear."

"Tell me what to do, Myra. I am so sorry. I feel like I let you all down."

"No, no, dear. No recriminations. I think you were set up. And the reason you were set up is because someone is watching all of us. They, whoever they are, know there is no one at Pinewood. This is what I want you to do. I'll call the limousine service Charles and I use and have them pick you up at your apartment. I want you to go to Pinewood and stay there. First, though, call the kennel people and have them bring the dogs back during the day. I want them there around the clock. Can you handle that, Isabelle?"

"Yes, Myra. I must be stupid. I thought it was just a random car-theft thing. They took everything, even my clothes. I'll call the kennel right now. When do you think you'll be home?"

"When you see me, Isabelle. I have a job to do. Bye, dear."

"What? What did she say? Tell me everything," Kathryn said.

Myra related the whole conversation, then said, "Pinewood is unattended at the moment. That worries me, Kathryn."

"It worries me, too," Kathryn agreed.

Eight

The caravan of luxury cars sped through the dark night toward Li's home. At some point during the evening, Li, with Charles's approval, had invited other guests to join him for an overnight stay in honor of his American guests. John Chai's father had declined the invitation, saying he had early-morning meetings scheduled, but his son John would be honored to attend. As it turned out, John drove himself there, with the other guests following in limousines and luxury cars.

Jay's passengers were tense and jittery.

"It's showtime, girls," Alexis kept saying. Every time she said it, Nikki's stomach heaved.

Charles opened one of the side compartments in the door to take out a pencil and paper. He scribbled furiously. *I can't reach Myra. No one is answering the phone at the farm. Isabelle isn't picking up either and for some reason my calls to Kathryn's cell get disconnected. I'm worried.*

116

Nikki reached for the pencil and paper. *Minor problem. They're big girls. We need to worry about the passenger in the car behind us. What made you decide to invite other people? How can we carry out our plans with so many people around?*

Charles replied immediately. *They're elderly and will retire early. It was Li's idea. He is our host. Trust us.*

The girls settled back in their seats, each busy with her own thoughts.

The silence was unnerving. Twice Charles rolled down the window, held his cell phone out and tried to call Myra. The call did go through but he clicked off when the answering machine came on again. The girls heard him muttering under his breath as the window rolled up, at which point he started to converse with Li in fluent Chinese.

The women bounced all over each other when the car finally came to a stop.

"Ladies! Ladies! A little decorum, please," Charles said quietly. "Li said drinks and sweet rice cakes will be served in his entertainment room. He has a new martial arts movie that will be shown if anyone is interested. For you young people, as Li so charmingly said, there is an American jukebox — a real Wurlitzer —

and a fully stocked bar. The La Ling sisters will retire when their parents do, so that won't pose a problem. Mr. Quon Zheyuan, a friend of John Chai's, will probably pass out shortly as he has already had far too much to drink. The man smokes a great deal of opium and anything he says is usually discounted. Wing Wu will be your only problem. He is a quasi-friend of John Chai. I'm sure you can entertain him when the time comes."

"Oh, it's raining," Alexis mumbled as she got out of the car and ran toward the house, Nikki and Yoko right behind her.

Inside the house, the women stepped aside to allow Li and his guests to precede them to the family area. A lot of bowing went on before the young people split off to be led to the entertainment room, where a small buffet table had been set up with classic American food and American beer in silver buckets full of ice.

Nikki tried to work some excitement into her voice. "Hey, guys, give us a few minutes to change out of these gowns. It's kind of hard to dance with so much material to drag around. In the meantime, help yourselves to the beer and food. Put on some lively music and we'll be back before you know it."

"I'll count the minutes," Chai said. Nikki wished she could wipe the smirk off his face with one good right hook. Instead, she smiled and winked. Wing Wu leered at her and said something to Chai that sounded suggestively dirty.

Yoko walked over to the pockmarked La Ling sisters and in Chinese invited both young women to join them. They declined and sat demurely, their hands folded in their laps. "They're no fun," Yoko said to Nikki and Alexis.

The three women raced down the long hall to their rooms where they changed into brightly colored spandex mini skirts with fishnet stockings and spike-heeled shoes. They chose sleazy-looking tops that showed off a generous portion of their bellies and a lot of cleavage.

Nikki looked at herself in the mirror. "Oh my God, I feel like a slut!"

"You look like one, too," Alexis laughed.

"Who is carrying the drugs?" Yoko asked.

"You are, darling," Alexis said as she held out six small white pills. "All you have to do is drop these in their beer bottles and within seconds they'll all be loose as a goose. We'll be dancing with each other because they won't be able to stand up.

When I tug on my ear, you do the deed. Our beer bottles are filled with apple juice and we're drinking Beck's. The boys are drinking Chinese beer. The La Ling sisters are probably guzzling hot tea, but who knows?"

"OK, girls, let's do it! We bound into the room like the Dallas Cowboys Cheerleaders when they hit the field at half-time. Show lots of teeth. Gyrate for all you're worth and, if you can, whisper dirty little ditties in their ears," Nikki said as she tugged on the spandex skirt.

Yoko opened the door, took a deep breath and raced down the hall. She threw open the door and made a grand entrance by somersaulting to the middle of the floor and then doing a neat split. Nikki's jaw dropped as she ran over to John Chai, reached down for his tie and pulled him to his feet. "Let's see your moves, Chinese boy!" she said as she rocketed to the middle of the dance floor. She was like a wild woman and all Chai could do was stare as he tried to get his feet to work.

The La Ling sisters tittered behind their hands. Alexis literally dragged Wing Wu to the dance floor. He was no match for the athletic long-legged beauty, but he did try. The La Ling sisters continued to titter.

Yoko looked down at Quon and flashed a smile. She bent low, looked into his vacant eyes, and whispered in his ear. "I'm a virgin! You wanna dance?"

Quon tried his best to focus on Yoko. He grinned as Yoko yanked him to his feet and literally dragged him out to the middle of the floor where Nikki and Alexis were whooping and hollering at the men who tried to keep up with them.

Wing Wu and Chai were sweating profusely — so profusely that their shirt fronts were drenched with sweat. Both men were staggering back toward their seats when the next record dropped on the turnstile.

"No, no! We came to dance! Take off your shirts. You take off yours and I'll take off mine! Woooooo, let's do it!" Alexis said, tugging on her ear, at which point Yoko gave Quon a stiff push. He folded like a wet noodle and slid across the polished dance floor to land near the La Ling sisters' feet. They tittered loudly and pretended not to notice the wild shenanigans around them. They were saved from further embarrassment when a servant came to escort them to their quarters. They shook their heads and spoke in hushed tones. The servant left quietly, leaving the sisters there.

The music ended. Gasping for breath, the couples headed for the table. Yoko was there in an instant, handing out bottles of beer. "Chug a lug!" she giggled.

Chai upended his bottle and was the first one done. He held it up triumphantly. Wu was a close second.

"And the winner is . . . John!" Nikki screamed as *Jambalaya* started playing on the Wurlitzer. "C'mon, let's dance!"

"I need to sit this one out," Chai mumbled.

"Chinese boy, you are disappointing me," Nikki said. She looked over at Wu and made a face. "What kind of party boys are you guys, anyway? C'mon, girls, let's dance by ourselves."

On the dance floor, Nikki shouted to Yoko so she could be heard over the music. "Go over to the sisters and ask them what's wrong with the boys. Sound disgusted. Play it up, Yoko. Shit, they're asleep. Keep dancing, Alexis, pretend you don't notice. Keep dancing. Five bucks says both of them will slide off those chairs within three minutes."

"That's a sucker bet," Alexis said as she twirled and whirled. "I'm too old for this, I'm getting tired."

"Tell me about it. My heart feels like it's

going to jump right out of my chest. Oops, there goes Wu Wing!"

"Wing Wu."

"Whatever. There goes Johnny. Oh, God, my hips and thighs are never going to be the same again."

Heaving and gasping, Alexis and Nikki made their way over to the La Ling sisters and Yoko. They bowed slightly to the sisters. "Yoko, ask the girls if we can get them some food. Tell them how disappointed we are in their friends. Do they speak any English?"

"They say no English. I am not so sure. They are not hungry but thank you for the offer. They wish me to tell you they adore your outfits and want to know where you got them. They want to know where you learned to dance like that."

"JC Penney for the clothes, Arthur Murray for the dancing." Alexis smiled. "What's with the guys?"

Yoko shrugged. "They say they are not so nice. They think it's funny that they fell asleep with three beautiful women like us wanting to dance with them. They have scurrilous reputations," Yoko translated.

The servant was back to escort the La Ling sisters to their quarters. "You come now. Father says now!" the servant said. Yoko translated again for the girls.

"OK, guess the party's over. We might as well go to bed, too," Yoko said in Chinese for the servant's benefit. She pointed to the three men and shrugged. The servant said something that sounded ugly.

"She said they should die in their sleep," Yoko said.

"Uh-huh," was all Alexis could say as she followed the sisters and the servant down the hall.

When they arrived at the atrium, the servant turned right to the east wing and the girls turned left to the west wing. Everyone bowed and waved goodbye.

Inside their room the women peeled off their clothes and donned jeans and sneakers. Their gear was packed within minutes. Alexis threw her red bag of tricks over her shoulder, opened the door, and looked both ways before she ran down the hall. Nikki and Yoko followed right behind her.

Back in the entertainment room they ran over to John Chai and propped him up on the chair. "God, this guy is so greasy I'm going to have to swab him down with alcohol. Keep your eyes on the other two. Charles said we have —" she looked at her watch — "exactly twenty-five minutes to transform this dude into an old man. Let's strip him down so we can get this kimono on him. Where the hell is the wheelchair?"

"It's under the buffet table," Yoko said. "I saw it when I was doctoring the beer. How long will they be asleep?"

"Three hours, maybe a little less. Just enough time to get out of here and on to the plane. Charles has John's documents. We got damn lucky with those sisters. Who would dispute anything they said? Hey, we left them here and went to bed. Perfect! Just perfect. Damn, Yoko, your aunts were right, this guy does have . . ."

"Keep your mind on your work. Who cares what size he is?" Nikki said, her voice so jittery that Alexis's eyebrows shot upward.

Yoko and Nikki watched as Alexis swiftly changed John Chai into a frail old Chinese man with straggly white hair and a long white mustache that looked like a dog's whiskers.

Charles and Li entered the room silently. They, too, stared in awe at Chai's altered appearance. "All we have to do is get him into the wheelchair and we're out of here," Nikki said. "What if some of the guests see us?"

"That's unlikely. Their tea was extra strong this evening. Gather up those empty beer bottles to bring with us. Empty out six more and set them on the table. We don't want anyone knowing you three were drinking apple juice, and there might be residue inside the men's bottles." Yoko hastened to follow Charles's orders.

"Is Mr. Li going with us, Charles?"

"Unfortunately, no. He said he wants to wake up in his own bed to greet his guests in the morning. He will, however, drive us to the airstrip. No more talk, it's time to leave. Time is of the essence. The Federal Aviation Administration granted me a small window of time. We have to be out of here on schedule. Li has arranged things to go smoothly. There will be no routines to follow, no stops for customs in this country. Hustle, girls."

Forty minutes later, everyone was aboard the Gulfstream. Chai was carried on board by Charles and Li. The two pilots looked the other way and chatted about the rainy weather. The two old friends shook hands. "If I —"

"Go, Sir Charles. I was glad to help."

Charles nodded and ran up the steps. A minute later, the aircraft door closed. By the time Charles buckled his seatbelt the

Gulfstream was taxiing down the runway. Outside, only pinpoints of red light could be seen in the distance. Li was already on his way home.

"Good luck, old friend," Charles whispered.

And then they were airborne. Their destination: the good old US of A. The women clapped their hands.

"My God! We did it! We really did it!" Nikki said.

"Myra is going to be so happy. Have you called her, Charles?"

"I've tried but I've been unsuccessful."

"I wonder where she is," Yoko mused.

"That's what I would like to know," Charles said.

Nikki looked at Charles. She didn't know if he was angry or worried. Probably both, she decided.

Nine

The frost on the ground crunched underneath the trio's feet as they made their way through the fragrant pine forest. The pungent scent was thick and heady. Jack could feel his sinuses starting to clog up. He looked down at his watch and then at Mark and Cyrus Conway. Both were giving him the evil eye. Right now both men hated him and he knew it.

Mark stomped his feet and rubbed his hands together. "This sucks, Jack! The last time I was out this early in a forest I was ten years old and in the Boy Scouts. How long is this going to take?"

"I think it's going to snow. It looks like snow. It even feels like snow," Conway said.

"Shut up, Cyrus. We're paying you double time to be here. Commune with nature. Be happy. Think about what you're going to do with all that overtime money. It's going to take as long as it takes." Jack lowered the high-powered binoculars. "The trainer is loading the dogs in the van. As soon as I vault the fence, I'll race over to the house, turn off the gates and you guys just hop over. Remember, time is crucial here. That guy is going to be sitting down at the end of the road waiting to see if anything happens. Don't even ask how I know this; I just do. Besides, it's what I would do if I was in his place. Where's the damn pole?"

Mark handed over a long bamboo pole and Jack vaulted the chain-link fence with ease.

"Show off," Mark mumbled as he tossed Jack's knapsack over the fence. Jack picked it up and sprinted toward the farmhouse. Within seconds the fence fizzled into safety mode. Within minutes, Mark and Cyrus were standing next to him just as he deactivated the alarm system in the house.

"Let's not waste any time. Come on, I want to show you where I saw that button. It's right there, on the fireplace. You know what else, I forgot to check the messages on the answering machine. Cyrus, you check the messages, but don't erase any of them. The machine is in the library. C'mon, Mark, you need to see this."

Both men were on their knees looking at

a small brass button imbedded in the carved rosette on the fireplace molding. Mark snapped the Polaroid and a blank picture shot out of the camera just as Conway burst through the door.

"That guy with the dogs is back and there's a limousine coming up the driveway. I could see from the window. I thought you said he was going to sit at the end of the driveway. He ain't sitting, Jack. He's here and he's got those damn dogs with him. C'mon, we have to get out of here!"

"Oh, shit!" Mark said as he raced to the kitchen. "We can't go out this way, they'll see us. You got a minute, maybe two before they figure out something's wrong with the gates. Say something, Jack, or I'm going to kill you right now!"

Jack ran to the laundry room and fished out some pantyhose that he'd seen lying around when he was disarming the alarm system. "I can't believe how clever I am sometimes!" He took out his pocket knife and cut the pantyhose into pieces. "Put these on your head and run like hell! We have a few minutes. C'mon, c'mon, you waiting for a bus or what? Do as I told you. OK, now run like those dogs have you in their sights, which they do. Jesus, will you listen to them! Go! Go! Go!" Jack bellowed.

The trio raced across the yard, down to the old barn and over the chain-link fence. They toppled over one another and then were up and running again. They could hear the dogs' shrill barks and howls coming from the house.

They sprinted to their cars and pulled out on to the road just as a string of patrol cars, sirens wailing, roared down the highway.

Mark wiped sweat from his forehead. "Tell me again what we accomplished, Jack. Because they are going to be the last words you ever utter. I'm killing you as soon as we get home."

Jack ignored him. "Where's Conway?"

"Two cars ahead of us. Can't you go any faster, Jack? The cops passed us; let 'er rip. I feel like a sitting duck."

"They didn't see us, Mark. Shit, we were so close. Ten more minutes, that's all it would have taken!"

"Think about this, you asshole. Let's just say that button did open on to a mysterious . . . what, Jack? A secret room? Stairs that lead to a secret tunnel? Then what? Just supposing you were right and we entered whatever is behind the fireplace and

131

the limo and the dogs arrived. What the hell would we have done? Picture this: the three of us carted off to jail. No money for bail. Our pictures on the front page. Are you listening to me, Jack?"

Jack shrugged. "Do you know if Conway took the tape from the answering machine? Take a look at the picture you snapped. Is the button visible?"

Mark looked down at the picture he was holding. "Yeah, you can see a button. For all the good it's going to do us. Where the hell are you going? This isn't the way to our apartment, and I have no idea if Conway took the tape or not. For all our sakes, I hope not."

"We're going to Georgetown to Nikki's town house. Then we're going to have breakfast, or I can make us breakfast at her house. I know where everything is."

"You're insane! Do you have a secret death wish?" Mark snarled.

"I'm not insane. I'm right. I knew — know — those women are out there breaking the law. I just proved it to you. Sometimes I am so smart I can't stand myself. And, no, I do not have a death wish. I also know we just blew our one and only opportunity to get inside that house. From here on in, good old Myra will probably hire a SWAT team to guard the place. More proof that something unlawful is going on. Bet you ten bucks that was the architect in the limo. Damn, why weren't we smart enough to put a bug in the phone?"

Mark clamped his lips shut. There was no sense wasting his breath talking to Jack. Jack had tunnel vision and a one-track mind when it came to the women of Pinewood.

They rode in silence until Jack finally said, "It's snowing! What are we doing for Thanksgiving, Mark?"

Mark gritted his teeth. It was indeed snowing. "What would you like to do for Thanksgiving, Jack?" he asked, but Jack didn't pick up on the heavy sarcasm. He was always amazed at how Jack could turn "it" off and go in another direction and then turn "it" back on and never miss a beat.

"Well, I don't think either one of us can cook up a full-scale dinner, so let's order from one of those places that do the whole thing. All you have to do is unwrap everything and set the table. We have to get some flowers for the table and some candles that smell. You're supposed to use a tablecloth on holidays with real napkins, not paper ones. Do you have a tablecloth and napkins, Mark?"

"Shut the hell up, Jack. Flowers, candles, tablecloths, what difference does it make, for God's sake?"

"The difference it makes is that it means we — me in particular — are not consumed by what's going on in our professional life. It means we can keep our private life separate, for example, on Thanksgiving, our private life, is separate from the women of Pinewood, our professional life. Call Conway again and give him Nik's address. Tell him to park wherever he can find a space. We're going to need that gizmo to disarm her security system."

"Do you know anything about Georgetown cops, Jack? They're mean as snakes."

"Kind of like you fibbies, huh?"

"Ex-fibbie, Jack. Yeah, like us. They kick ass first and take names later."

"Mark, Mark, Mark, first they have to find our asses before they can kick them. Nik is always someplace. That means we have a clear shot at her town house. No one is going to call and complain. You need to relax or you're going to get high blood pressure."

Mark clamped his lips shut, his eyes straight ahead. He marveled at Jack's good fortune in finding a parking spot on the crowded street. He watched as Conway parked three spaces down. If he was doing the driving, with his usual luck, he'd have had to park a mile away. Jack was right about the blood pressure, too. He really did need to relax more.

Jack picked the lock on Nikki's door within seconds and had the alarm deactivated in no time. "Come on in, boys, and I'll whip us up some breakfast, but first I want to check out a few things. Nik keeps a little office upstairs. I want to go through her things. Mark, see if you can lift anything of importance off her computer. Conway, set the table and get the stuff ready. Scrambled eggs, bacon, whatever you can find. Use her best dishes. This is a party."

"I am personally going to sign your commitment papers when they cart you off," Mark said.

Jack laughed all the way up the stairs. He had a bad moment when he saw Nikki's neat, tidy bedroom. It smelled so much like her that his eyes started to water. He was stunned to see a picture of the two of them on her dresser. Suddenly he wanted to cry the way he'd cried when he was a little kid. He tried to shake off the feeling

135

but his eyes stayed moist. He knew Mark was pretending not to see what he was going through.

"OK, let's get with it."

One of the police officers led Isabelle to the side. "Tell me one more time exactly what you saw and the time you saw it."

Isabelle kneaded her hands. "I came out here in a limousine. You already spoke to the driver. We were right behind the man from the kennel. I got out of the limo when the trainer got out. The gate was dead, the power off. When I left here a few days ago, the power was on and the alarm was on in the house. The trainer said it was on when he left a little while ago. I've been . . . been house-sitting. I wasn't able to get out here yesterday because I had car trouble. Mrs. Rutledge called the limousine company and had them pick me up. When the trainer finally managed to pry open the gates enough so we could slip through, I saw that the lock on the kitchen door had been picked. I'm assuming it was picked, because I locked it when I left. I set the alarm, too."

"When did you see the three figures running away?"

"When the trainer was trying to pry

open the gates. The dogs were going crazy and it had just started to snow. All I know is there were three of them. They had something over their heads. I don't know this for sure, but it looked like . . . like pantyhose or something sheer like that. Whatever it was, it was flesh-colored. Like I said, it was snowing, the flakes were kind of swirling around making it hard to see. I wasn't wearing my glasses. I need them for distance but since I wasn't driving, I didn't have them on. Maybe the trainer could see better than me."

"Was anything taken from the house?"

"I don't know. I don't live here. It doesn't look like it to me but I can't be sure. I told you, I'm just house-sitting till Mrs. Rutledge gets back."

The officer narrowed his eyes slightly. "Where exactly is Mrs. Rutledge? When will she be back? Do you have a way to get in touch with her?"

Isabelle pretended to sigh mightily. "Mrs. Rutledge doesn't share her personal comings and goings with me. I'm a paid employee. I'm not sure, but I think she's due back late tonight or tomorrow. No, I do not have a number where she can be reached. It's not like there are small children here or pets where something could go awry. I told you, I'm just watching the house."

"Those dogs out there . . . what's that all about?"

"Officer, I simply don't know. I guess Mrs. Rutledge values her privacy. They're usually just here at night. You'll have to talk to the trainer if you want to know more about those dogs. Personally, they scare the crap out of me. Is there anything else, Officer? Excuse me, the phone is ringing."

Isabelle grappled with the wall phone as an arctic blast of air swirled into the kitchen. She didn't offer a greeting until the door closed behind the officer. Her "hello" was cautious, even breathless. "Charles, thank God! It's Isabelle." She quickly related the past events. "You sound so far away. What a silly thing to say. Of course you're far away. Exactly where are you, Charles?"

"Airborne. We're on our way home. I don't want you to say anymore on the phone, Isabelle. I've been trying to reach Myra. Will you put her on please, Isabelle?"

"Myra isn't here, Charles. She went on the road with Kathryn. I think it was a last-minute decision on her part because when they finally called me they were already headed cross-country. Is there anything you want me to do?"

"No. Don't leave the farm. Keep the alarm on. I can't think of a better deterrent than those dogs. We should be home in the early hours of the morning." The conversation turned to the mundane as Charles rattled off a grocery list for their Thanksgiving dinner. Isabelle dutifully wrote it all down and promised to call in the food order. She was shaking when she hung up the phone.

She ran into the laundry room. She needed to do something normal. Laundry was normal. Making coffee was normal. Ordering groceries was normal. She turned on the brand new turbo washer, added soap, bleach and softener in the appropriate dispensers and started to throw in the dirty clothes she'd brought with her days ago. It finally dawned on her that the pantyhose she had meant to hand wash were missing. Suddenly she didn't feel like doing any laundry, too rattled to put the obvious two and two together. Coffee seemed like a better idea.

Isabelle looked around the kitchen, panic written all over her face. When she'd left the other day she'd cleaned out the coffee pot and pulled the plug, but it was plugged in now. There were ground coffee beans in the wire basket and leftover coffee in the pot. Whoever had been in the house had certainly made themselves at home. Who? The people who had been watching the house from the forest? Jack Emery and his friends? If it was Jack Emery, that had to mean they were still watching the house and the comings and goings of all of them. Suddenly her car break-in made sense. The theft of her stuff and her cell phone made even more sense. Myra was right; she'd been set up.

Isabelle cleaned the pot and made coffee because she didn't know what else to do. While it dripped, she walked from room to room, careful to avoid going near the fireplace. Charles had warned them all about the high-tech telescopic lenses that could see through anything but steel. She jolted backward in the library when she saw the little cover on the answering machine flipped up. She knew what she was seeing but she wiggled her fingers around the opening anyway. The mini cassette was gone. That's when her knees gave out and she had to sit down.

"Oh, God, Myra, why didn't you ever get voicemail?" She wondered if the phone was bugged. She almost jumped out of her skin when it rang. Should she answer it? Of course she should. She just had to be careful what she said.

"Hello, Rutledge residence. This is Isabelle Flanders."

"Hey, guess who?" came the cheery greeting. "Julia!"

"I'm not in the mood for games, whoever you are, so just hang up and free up this line. There are police here and they might want to use the phone." Isabelle hoped Julia would understand that she couldn't talk to her.

"I'm so sorry. I must have dialed the wrong number," the voice said before the connection was broken.

Isabelle slammed the phone into the cradle as if it had suddenly turned into a poisonous snake.

Back in the kitchen she poured coffee. She gulped at it, her eyes watering as it burned her tongue and throat. She didn't care. She looked down at Julia's plant and was happy to see that it was thriving under the skylight. She wished she could have mentioned it to Julia. She shrugged. Julia would be here for Thanksgiving; she could see it for herself.

Outside, the dogs patrolled the grounds.

She was stunned to see that it was still snowing. By craning her neck, she could see that the trainer had left the new barn door open for the dogs. The barn was heated and Myra had told her that the dog beds, water and food were set out by the trainer every day. The dogs looked sleek and deadly, but she also knew if they trapped a quarry they would sit and hold.

Suddenly it dawned on her that some people out there were wearing her panty hose on their heads. How weird was that? She started to laugh, but her laughter was hysterical rather than amused.

Ten

Myra leaned her head back so that Murphy, his paws on her shoulders, could nestle his big head on her. He liked nuzzling her neck and did it periodically during the long trip. He had, after all, given up his shotgun seat for her. "I really do think this wonderful animal likes me," Myra said. "I'm going to give him a special treat when we get to the house." Murphy thumped her shoulder in approval.

"So, Myra, do you think you could make a living on the road? You ride shotgun real good. I thought Murphy would be upset giving up his seat, but I think he likes it that you're sitting there."

"Dear, one time was enough. I wasn't too much of a drag, was I?"

"Lady, you saved me a bundle of money. Murphy might have gotten wise to those thieves, but unfortunately he can't talk. I owe you for that, Myra."

"You don't owe me a thing, dear. I had

the time of my life. We do stink, though. I think Charles would say we're *gamey*. I don't think I ever went three whole days without bathing in my entire life. Everything was such an experience. I had a lovely time. How will we get this pine resin off our hands?"

"By scrubbing our skin off, that's how. Nail polish remover will take the worst of it off. You better move your head. In about five minutes, Murphy is going to spot the turn-off that will take us to McLean. He knows the way, believe it or not. He's going to bounce all over the place, so be prepared." Myra leaned forward just moments before Murphy belly-crawled over the seat and Myra's shoulder. He barked one shrill burst before his big paws slammed against the window. "Told you," Kathryn laughed.

Myra giggled. Kathryn thought it the most endearing sound she'd ever heard.

"I hope Charles is at Pinewood. Do you think it's too soon, Kathryn?"

Kathryn shrugged. "I'm thinking sometime tomorrow. I say that because I know Charles and the others want to be home for Thanksgiving. We have to be patient."

Ten minutes later Myra gasped. "My goodness, Isabelle must be having a party! Every light in the house is on. I do hope she wasn't afraid being in the house alone. You have the dog whistle, don't you?"

"Yep, it's been hanging on my neck for days now. Two sharp blasts and the dogs return to the barn! No cars, so that means Isabelle doesn't have company." The gates swung open, allowing Kathryn to drive her eighteen-wheeler through them. She rolled down her window and gave two sharp blasts on the special whistle. In the headlights both women could see the dogs racing to the barn. The gates closed just as Kathryn cut the engine on the rig. Murphy was the first one out, Myra second, and finally Kathryn.

"I hope it snows all night," Myra said. "I do love waking up to a winter wonderland. It will be nice if we have snow for Thanksgiving. Over the hills and through the woods to Myra's house we go," she sang. "Would you look at me! Charles would be aghast if he could see me right now."

Arm in arm, the two women walked across the concrete apron and up the steps to the kitchen door. Kathryn rang the bell. Isabelle came running, a look of relief on her face when she saw who was there.

"I need a beer," Myra said. "Truckers drink a lot of beer. Did you know that,

Isabelle? I had a marvelous time. Did Charles call? Is there a reason why the house is so lit up, dear? OK, chug a lug! Later, I'll show you how to play quarters. The life of a trucker is so interesting. I have six — that's six, Isabelle — invitations to the Truckers' Ball. I'm going, too. See this shirt? I earned it! Just ask Kathryn. Someday you have to ride shotgun with Kathryn. It's an exhilarating experience. Now, tell us what's been going on." Myra stopped babbling, suddenly all business as she swigged from her beer bottle.

Isabelle brought them up to date.

"I'm looking forward to seeing Julia. I can't believe the girls and Charles are actually on their way back to us. Nothing else matters, not even Jack Emery and his henchmen. I'm not going to give him another thought. I'm sorry about your car, Isabelle. I'll speak to Charles about replacing it. Now, you girls sit here and talk girl-talk while I take a nice long bubble bath. I think I'll just take another beer with me. You were right, Kathryn, it grows on you. The beer, I mean. Goodnight, girls. If Charles arrives, please wake me."

"You got it, Myra," Kathryn said, offering up a salute. "Sleep tight."

When Myra was out of earshot, Kathryn leaned across the table. "I swear to God, Isabelle, she was the best damn shotgun I ever rode with. I wish you could have seen her. She was on the horn and picked up the lingo like that," Kathryn said, snapping her fingers. "She loved the greasy food at the truck stops, going for seconds if you can believe that. She saved my ass at the depot when she overheard three thieves ripping me off. Then, when we got to this Mom and Pop place in North Carolina, Mom and Pop didn't have anyone to unload the trees so Myra and I did it. The lady didn't bat an eye. She's something else. The whole trip, all she kept saying was she wished Charles could see her. You know what, I wished he could have seen her, too." Kathryn suddenly switched gears. "So someone took the answering machine tape *and* your pantyhose. Perverts. The world's full of them."

Isabelle shrugged. "I think you should go to bed, Kathryn, you look exhausted. I'll stay up because I'm not sleepy. We can talk in the morning."

"I am tired. I gotta take a shower first, though. I think I'm even *scuzzier* than Myra. See you in the morning. Be sure to wake me if anything happens. I'll leave

Murphy down here with you. Night, Isabelle."

"Wait a minute, Kathryn. Did Myra talk about . . . *that guy?* When I told her just now that they were on their way back *with him,* she didn't seem overly excited."

"Yeah, I noticed that, too. She's on a high, Isabelle, and hasn't come down to earth yet. She had the time of her life on the road. You have to admit, life out here on the farm is pretty dull even with all of us and . . . what we're doing. The hiatus between missions is months. She must get terribly bored, but I can tell you, her adrenalin sure was flowing these past few days. We'll see tomorrow when Charles and the others get back. I'm dead on my feet. See you later. Murph, stay with Isabelle."

Isabelle stood by the kitchen window for a long time, staring out at the falling snow. Finally she tore her gaze away and said, "Let's go watch some stupid show on television, Murphy. I built a nice fire a little while ago. I even put a basket of dog bones in there by your bed."

Gentleman that he was, Murphy waited for Isabelle to lead the way.

Charles tossed aside the magazine he was reading, unbuckled his seatbelt and got up. "We're ninety minutes outside of Baltimore-Washington Airport. Alexis, it's time to get ready. How's our guest?"

Nikki shrugged. "Well, he looks like he's dead, but he isn't. He stirred a little while ago but then went back to sleep. I think he's going to be wild when he finally wakes up."

Charles looked down at the shackles binding the man's feet to his hands by way of a chain. "I imagine so, but he isn't going anywhere. I tried to call Li but there's no answer at his house. I'm concerned."

Nikki could only nod.

Yoko walked forward. "Is our guest awake?"

"He's starting to come around. Another few minutes. Alexis, are you ready?" Charles asked.

"You bet," Alexis said, opening her red bag. "By the way, whose idea was it to dress him in that kimono? I say we just cut it off, less of a struggle." She fished around in the bag and withdrew a pair of yellow-handled scissors and started to cut away the silk kimono that was embroidered with fire-eating dragons.

"He's wearing a black silk Speedo. Not much there," Nikki said, tongue in cheek. "Be sure to tell your aunts they were right. Seeing is believing," she said.

John Chai's eyes popped open. He struggled to focus. When he saw the four faces peering down at him, he flinched. A nanosecond later he realized he wasn't wearing anything but his underwear. Another nanosecond later he seemed to realize he was on an airplane. So far there was no fear in his eyes. He made a move to get up, only to realize he was shackled to the seat. Obscenities spewed from his mouth. Yoko covered her ears.

"Hi there, Chinese boy," Nikki said cheerfully. "I gotta tell you, your fame as a party boy was grossly exaggerated. Well, we're going to fix that right now."

More obscenities followed, this time in English. "My father will have you killed for this. My family has royal blood. You can't kidnap me!"

Nikki rolled her eyes. "Hey, Chinese boy, we already kidnapped you. Look at yourself, look at us. We're in charge here. Don't insult us."

A flicker of fear showed on Chai's face. "What do you want? How much money for my safe return?"

"There's not enough money in the world to buy your way out of this situation," Charles said.

"Then what is it you want from me?

150

Are you after my father? Why are you doing this? I haven't done anything to you."

"No, just you. Your father and his wealth are of no concern to us," Nikki said and grinned.

This time there was more than a flicker of fear in Chai's eyes. "Where are you taking me?"

"The land of the free and the brave. The good old US of A., Johnny. We're about seventy minutes outside of Washington, DC. We'll be making our descent soon. You remember Washington, don't you, Chinese boy? You were a regular on the party circuit, weren't you? Twenty-four-seven was the way I heard it. Guess what, those party days are over now. Now you're going to party with us."

Fear galloped across Chai's features. The reality of what was happening finally kicked in. He started to babble, first in Chinese and then in English.

"Oh, will you just shut up already! You talk more than an all-night disk jockey. You're here, we're here, and you aren't going anywhere, *Mister* Chai," Nikki said.

"OK, I'm ready," Alexis trilled as she dragged her red bag over to the seat where Chai was sitting. "First we dress him. Just looking at him offends me. Here," she said, tossing a pair of cheap black cotton trousers and a long-sleeved black Mandarin shirt at Yoko.

A whispered conversation between the women and Charles followed. Finally, Charles reached into a first-aid kit and withdrew a hypodermic. Before Chai could protest, the syringe made contact with his arm. "One minute and we can release his shackles. Be quick, Alexis. I gave him just enough to keep him out for two hours. He'll be half-awake but very groggy when we land. He'll probably be wide awake by the time we reach Pinewood. I'm going forward to talk to the pilots. Like I said, be quick."

The women obliged while John Chai slept the sleep of the dead.

Chai was unshackled and dressed in minutes, just in time for Alexis to warm her spirit gum and latex. Yoko held the mega-wattage flashlight so that Alexis could see what she was doing. The first thing she did was shave off Chai's shiny black hair. Nikki scooped it up as fast as it dropped to the floor. Then she plastered, patted, poked and sanded. A glop of glue went on to his head. Alexis smoothed it out and added straggly white hairs from a plastic bag. "When the glue dries it will look like his bare scalp shining through."

The girls marveled at the expertise, which she'd garnered while working with Little Theater. Within minutes, Chai took on the appearance of a wizened ninety-year-old man. Another glop of glue then went over Chai's upper lip. More straggly hairs were stuck into the glue and trailed down both sides of his lips. Finally a sad, sparse-looking goatee was added.

Alexis threw her hands in the air. "Ladies, I give you my version of Fu Manchu. Whatcha think? Oops, I forgot something." The girls watched in wonderment as Alexis pulled out a padded shoulder brace, similar to what football players wore, and attached it around Chai's shoulders. "It's heavy, weighted. He'll be stoop-shouldered. I'm going to attach another one to his waist that will hang down to his buttocks. He'll be so groggy he won't understand why he can't stand up straight. We want him to look old, bowed, miserable, and there will be no doubt that he is in physical pain."

Charles walked down the aisle and gasped. "Alexis, my dear, you are without doubt a master of disguise. I would never in a million years recognize John Chai.

The last thing we have to do is take our seats and prop up Mr. Chai so the co-pilot can take a video of us all chatting. The time and the date will be on the video. Should we ever need to prove who was on this flight with us, Mr. Chai's papers say he is a poor farmer from Aberdeen named Gan Jun that we are bringing to America to have a kidney transplant. There will be a record of Mr. Jun being admitted to Georgetown Hospital, thanks to Julia's efforts all the way from Switzerland. No further information will be given out. In two days' time, Mr. Jun will be discharged to an American family where he will receive dialysis at home until a kidney donor can be found. From there, he will drop off the face of the earth. Here comes the co-pilot. Smile prettily and look concerned over our fellow passenger. The video has sound, so be careful. Just chat normally."

Charles complimented them all when the taping session was over. "We may have one small problem with Mr. Chai when the plane lands. I'm thinking the pilots can carry him down the air stair, at which point we'll put him in the portable wheelchair. There's no way we can let him stumble down the steps. We'll be landing in just a few minutes. The wheels are down. The co-pilot will continue to video us as we take him to the car. I want all of you to look solicitous. Another hour and we'll be home safe and sound."

The relief was so apparent on the women's faces that Charles chuckled. "You're the best. I wish I had all of you on my side years ago when I was an active agent with MI6."

"Charles, that's the nicest thing you ever said to us," Nikki crowed.

"We couldn't have done it without you," Alexis said.

"You're wonderful, Charles," Yoko smiled. "Truly, truly, wonderful!"

Eleven

Jack Emery smacked his lips as he finished the last of his coffee. "I have to say, gentlemen, that was one of the best breakfasts I've had in a long time. I guess we should be going since we didn't come up with anything in Nik's records. Seems to me she's dividing her time between here and Pinewood. For a while she was living out there full-time. I think when nothing is going on, she stays here. When they're doing whatever the hell it is they're doing, she stays at Pinewood. To me, that means dirty work is afoot."

"That's a brilliant deduction, Jack," Mark said. "Now what?"

"Now we sit back and wait to see what our new operative comes up with. He should have arrived at his post —" Jack looked at his watch — "twenty minutes ago. Three hours on, three off."

"We're running out of guys who are willing to sit up in a tree, Jack. Look outside, it's snowing like hell."

"You're a fusspot, Mark. Those pine trees are the best shelter there is. The Indians used to cover themselves with pine boughs to keep warm. I think it's the resin or something. If the guys wear the body warmers, they can do a three-hour stretch, no sweat. If it's the money, don't pay me and use my share for the stakeouts. You guys go on home and get ready for Thanksgiving. I'll stay here to clean up and take a cab back to the apartment. Mark, see what you can come up with at the airport. See if any flight plans were filed for the Gulfstream. I don't see any of the women, especially Myra, being away from Pinewood for Thanksgiving. Conway, rest up so you can relieve the guy who's out there now. Call Garrity to replace you when you leave."

Jack poured himself the last of the coffee after Mark and Conway left. His shoulders slumped. Now that he was alone he didn't have to pretend for the guys. He hated giving up, but it didn't seem like he had any other options at the moment. If he had had ten more minutes at Pinewood, he was absolutely certain he would have found the proof he needed to make a case against the women. Ten more minutes. Then again, maybe Mark was right. What good was all the proof in the world if his ass was lounging in jail?

Jack finished his coffee, got up and walked through the town house. He touched this and that, memories surfacing which he tried quickly to bury.

If you can't beat them, join them. Now where the hell did that thought come from? In the living room Jack sat down on the sofa where he and Nik had slept, cuddled, made love. They'd been so happy, so in love. That wasn't to say they didn't have spats from time to time; they did. The making up, the promises not to act like that again, had been glorious. He'd given her a ring. Why didn't she return it? She wasn't the kind of girl to keep it for spite or to hock. His spirits lifted a little. Maybe keeping it meant she hadn't wiped him totally out of her life. Right, and pigs fly.

He got up and walked around. He stopped at the mantel to look at the pictures. Barbara and Nik; Nik and Myra; Nik, Myra and Charles. Big pictures, little pictures, old pictures, recent pictures. There were none of him on the mantel. It didn't matter, he still had the place of honor in her bedroom. If she hated him, Nik would have trashed the picture.

In his heart he couldn't fault Nikki for

loving Myra. He loved his own mother just as much. The only difference was, his mother lived in another world due to her medical condition. Myra was still vital, still living in this world.

Everything had changed between them when Barbara was killed by that diplomat's son. A son with diplomatic immunity.

Son of a bitch!

The sun was nudging the horizon when the black car pulled up to the gates of Pinewood. Charles pressed in the code, reached up to the visor for the dog whistle, and blew two sharp blasts.

The group took a minute to admire what nature had created overnight. The two-inch layer of snow clung to the trees and ground.

"Norman Rockwell," Nikki said. "Can our guest make it on his own, Charles?"

"I don't think so. I'll help him. If you don't mind, carry in your own bags. You can leave mine and I'll get it later. I see Kathryn is here. Julia should be arriving by mid-afternoon. I made arrangements for a car service to pick her up. Look lively, Mr. Jun," Charles growled under his breath.

The girls looked around as they flanked the couple heading toward the house. Chai did indeed look ancient as he tottered alongside Charles.

On the second floor, Myra stirred beneath her nest of covers. She'd been so tired when she finally went to bed that she'd forgotten to close the draperies. Now a blinding whiteness assailed her from the wrap-around windows. She closed her eyes as she mentally counted her various aches and pains. The moment she heard Charles's voice, she swung her legs over the side of the bed. She was still tying the belt around her robe as she ran down the hall to the staircase in her bare feet.

"Charles, you're home!" she trilled as her aching bones protested her quick movements. When she realized the voices were coming from the kitchen, she stopped a moment to smooth down her springy gray curls. "Oh, who cares what I look like so early in the morning," she muttered as she pushed at the swinging door.

Myra ran to Charles, hugged him tightly before she embraced each of the women. "I was so worried. You're home, thank God. I thought . . . You should introduce me to your friend, Charles," she said, noticing the old gentleman for the first time. Her eyes were full of questions. Finally, she couldn't stand it a moment longer. "What went wrong? I knew it was impossible. I had such high hopes."

"Myra, dear, listen to me," Charles said.

"It's all right, Charles. I'm not blaming you. We all knew it was an impossible mission. Another time," she said, her eyes brimming with tears.

"Myra, allow me to present Gan Jun, also known as John Chai. Alexis fixed him up for security reasons. We didn't fail, dear. Everything went off without a hitch. We were there, now we're here. I'm taking our guest down to the tunnels. Is there anything you want to say before we leave?"

Myra stared at the man who had taken Barbara's life and that of her unborn child. Somewhere in the back of her mind she had a litany of things she wanted to say but none of them would make it to her tongue. Her eyes spewed hatred — hatred that didn't register with John Chai. She shook her head, waving the two men off. Yoko helped her over to the table, where she sat down.

"What should I have done, girls? I didn't know what to do. It's not like there's some kind of protocol to follow. In my heart I think I thought you'd fail to bring him here. I didn't let myself get my hopes up. Now that he's here, in my very own house,

I have to rethink . . . think . . . decide . . . I might need a little more time. He's here in my house! He was just standing in front of me. Does he know why he's here?"

"He's been doped up, Myra. All he knows, if he remembers, is that he's in the United States. We didn't tell him anything. We thought you would want to be the one to explain to him why he's here and what we plan to do to him. Listen, if you all don't mind, I need to get a few hours' sleep," Nikki said.

"Run along, dear. You, too, Alexis. Yoko, are you staying over?"

"Just long enough to get some sleep. I must return home to my husband, but I will come back."

Myra sat alone at the table as Isabelle set about making breakfast and coffee.

"There must be something wrong with me, Isabelle. I should know what I'm feeling but I don't. I should know what to do but I don't. I had that one moment of pure hatred and then . . . and then it went away. For so long all I thought about was getting even with him, making him pay for what he'd done. Now that the time is actually here, I don't know . . . I just don't know." Myra looked down at the toast Isabelle put in front of her. She could see it was just the way she liked it: warm, the butter melted, with a light layer of blackberry jam. She wondered if it would stick in her throat if she tried to eat it. She opted to sip at the coffee in her cup. "This is good, Isabelle. Thank you."

Isabelle nodded as she sat down across from Myra. "Where . . . where did Charles take that man, Myra?"

"I'm assuming into the tunnels. There are one or two little rooms, cells actually, at the very end of the first tunnel. I used to hang bells where all the tunnels connected so Barbara and Nikki wouldn't get lost. I was always close at hand. Charles shored them up over the years. For the life of me, I can't remember why he did that. Maybe so Barbara and Nikki's children could play there someday.

"Anyway, the two cells have bars just like jails do. I used to say I'd like to see John Chai in one of those cells so he could rot and die there. I was so full of hate back then. I guess I still am."

Myra looked up to see Charles standing in the doorway. "Our guest is in residence, Myra. The drugs are starting to wear off so he's going to be rather unhappy." He picked up Myra's toast and started to eat it. Isabelle handed him a cup of steaming coffee. Myra thought he looked more tired than she'd ever seen him.

Normally Myra was never at a loss for words, but for some reason she felt like her mouth was stuffed with peanut butter. All she could think to say was, "Thank you, dear. I . . . I need to . . . Oh, Charles, I don't know what I need to do. Just sit here for a while, I guess. Go to bed and get some rest. We'll all be here when you wake up. Shoo," she said, trying to be light-hearted.

Charles leaned over to kiss Myra's cheek. She reached up and patted his hand. She then pulled his hand closer and kissed it.

She grappled for something to say after Charles left the room. "Did you place the grocery order, Isabelle? Maybe we should think about doing some cooking. Charles is going to be rather busy so I guess it will be up to us. I can't believe tomorrow is Thanksgiving. Well, I certainly have a lot to be thankful for this year, don't I?"

Isabelle poured more coffee. She knew Myra was just talking to hear her own voice. She couldn't help but wonder how she would act and feel when it was finally her time to right the wrong done to her. "I'm not much of a cook, Myra."

Myra offered up a wry smile. "Don't tell

anyone, but I'm not much of a cook, either. Like it's a secret!" Both women laughed. "I think it's time for me to shower and dress. Is there anything you want me to do, Isabelle?"

"You go ahead, Myra. I have some laundry to fold. I need to feed Murphy, too. I do know how to make stuffing for the turkey. I can do that. It will mean less for us to do later. Or I can make muffins out of a box for when the others wake up."

"That sounds splendid, Isabelle. I just love Murphy. Make him a big hamburger. He deserves it. He really hates dog food. Sometimes I think he thinks he's human," Myra said vaguely before she left the kitchen.

Investigator Conway adjusted the zoom lens on his camera, eyed his subjects, and pressed the button, not once, not twice, but three times. He was confident he'd gotten a clear shot of the old Asian man dressed in black who could barely walk. He clicked again and again as the women moved to withdraw their bags from the trunk. The minute the group was out of sight and in the house, he yanked his cell phone out of his pocket. His voice was excited as he related what he'd just done.

"What do you want me to do, Mark? Listen, man, it's cold as hell out here. These people don't look like they're going anywhere. If you want me to take the film to one of those one-hour places, I can do that. Then how about if I conduct surveillance out on the road? I think they're snuggled in, man."

"Yeah, OK. Call me when you get the photos back. Either Jack or I will come out and pick them up. How old is old, Conway?"

"He looked old to me. Older than my grandfather and he's in his mid-seventies. He had little bits of long straggly hair, a stringy mustache that trailed down to his neck, and a goatee. He was stooped over pretty bad. He had trouble walking. Like maybe ninety. I don't know, Mark. The big guy had to help him walk. He looked sick and frail to me. Can I go now?"

"Sure, but stay in touch."

The women were busy in the kitchen, cooking and chatting, when Charles entered at midday. He looked rested and freshly shaven. He even smelled good. He eyed the disarray in the kitchen and winced.

"It's all right, Charles, the girls know

what they're doing. We're making mince pies and a pumpkin one for you. From scratch, dear. Yoko will come back in the morning. Now, tell us, what should we do in regard to . . . to . . . *that man.*"

"I want you all to stop what you're doing, turn off the stove and come with me. It's time for you to meet John Chai. We can introduce Julia to Mr. Chai later on when she gets here. It's time, Myra."

Myra started to tremble as she rubbed at her arms, her face full of panic. "You . . . you won't open the cell door, will you, Charles?"

"No, Myra, I won't open the cell door. By now, our guest should be completely lucid." He reached into the refrigerator for a bottle of water. He snatched a piece of stale bread from the counter before he led the parade to the living room. He counted down slowly, then pressed the hidden button in the rosette. One by one the women, all silent now, followed him down the steep steps to the tunnels instead of turning right to the opening that would have taken them to the war room.

They walked for what seemed like a long time. Twice, Myra reached up to ring the old bells hanging overhead. Even though they were rusty, the sound was as clear and pure as the day she'd hung them up for the girls. Tears blurred her vision. Charles reached behind him to take her hand.

The high beam on his flashlight cut a bright swath as Charles suddenly came to an abrupt stop. He turned off the flashlight. Attached to one of the beams he'd used to shore up this particular section of the tunnel was a high-voltage battery-operated lamp. The women crowded around to peer into the dark, dank cell. John Chai bounded over to the steel bars and kicked them. He cursed, first in English and then in Chinese.

They all ignored him. "Ladies, allow me to introduce you to John Chai, also known as Gan Jun." The man inside spit at them.

Myra could feel herself shaking from head to toe. This was the moment she had thought would never come. The moment she had dreamed of. The moment which she'd promised her daughter would perhaps come someday, without truly believing it. She felt a light, feathery touch on her shoulder. Thinking it was one of the girls, she turned around. No one was standing near her, they'd all moved to the side to give her center stage.

"You can handle this. There are no rules where he's concerned. The bells sound

the same. This is where he belongs. Take a deep breath. I'm right here next to you, Mom."

Twelve

Jack Emery stared down at the pictures in his hands. Who the hell was this old guy? Why did Charles Martin, Nikki, the Asian woman and the black girl go to China? Did it take four people to bring back one old guy? Conway said the old guy could walk but with difficulty. None of the women — or Charles, for that matter — had a medical background.

He held the pictures out to Mark. "What do you make of these?"

Mark opened his desk drawer to pull out a magnifying glass. He held it over the pictures as he stared down at them. "Looks like some sick old guy to me. We're talking *old* here, Jack. Maybe the people of Pinewood are a bunch of humanitarians and brought the old man here for some kind of medical treatment. That would be my guess. What's your best guess?"

Jack chewed on his lower lip. He knew that when he told Mark what his best guess was, Mark would throw up his hands in disgust and probably boot his ass all the way to the Georgia border. "I think this old guy," he said, tapping the picture in his hand, "has something to do with the kid who killed Myra's daughter. That's what I think, Mark. I think those ladies went to China with Martin's connections — and we know Martin has connections. I still have the scars to prove it. I think they snatched the old guy — maybe he's the kid's father or grandfather — in hopes of having them surrender the kid. The kid — I don't know why I keep calling him a kid, he's in his late twenties or early thirties — can't come back to the States. If he does, the authorities can go after him legally. We both know he's never coming back here. At least not under his own power. I don't care if you think I'm nuts or not. Those women at Pinewood are not humanitarians, trust me on that."

"Well, the guy in the picture is *not* Chai's father. The guy's father is a fat little toad of a man with a slicked-back hairdo. He's in his fifties. I have pictures of him in my file. He's not the grandfather either, because he's dead. Chai has one sister who lives in Beijing, but she's young, in her early twenties. There are, of course, hundreds of aunts, uncles, cousins. Think about it, Jack, why would they snatch some old guy and bring him here to . . . what?"

"Ransom. The old guy for the young guy? Why not? They can't get to the young guy any other way. Myra wants someone to pay for her daughter's death. I don't think either one of us can fault her for that. OK, having Conway out on the road isn't going to do us any good. He needs to get back up in the tree. If he won't or can't do it, I will. I want to know the second that old geezer makes a move. If he leaves the house I want to know where the hell he goes and who's taking him wherever he's going."

"Shit, Jack, tomorrow is Thanksgiving. I thought we were going to do dinner and take the day off."

"Yeah, yeah, that was the plan when we talked about it. Things changed, as you can see. Get hold of Conway and tell him to get his tail back in that tree. Line up Garrity and what's-his-name. I'm thinking that crafty bunch of women are hoping Thanksgiving will throw us off. Trust me, they're going to make a move. I feel it in my gut."

Mark eyed his friend. He was probably

right. Jack did have uncanny instincts. He nodded. "Just so you know, buddy, this is going to seriously deplete our operating expenses."

"I know. I'm prepared to eat macaroni and cheese for the rest of my life with maybe a little peanut butter thrown in. I'll do my own laundry, collect aluminum cans if I have to. I'll take my turn out in the tree."

"Yeah, I guess I'll take a turn up in the damn tree to keep expenses down. You know we're going to get our asses in a sling, right, Jack?"

"Probably, but I'm not going to worry about it or go down without a fight," Jack said.

"Does this mean we're not ordering a takeout Thanksgiving dinner? You know, in the spirit of keeping expenses down?"

"That's what it means. Spam sandwiches for us. I'll make it up to you, Mark. Now, let's put our heads together and try to get one step ahead of those foxy ladies and their fearless MI6 guy. My gut tells me we're about to get up to bat and are going to kick some serious ass."

"Man, I hope to hell you're right, Jack. I don't ever want to go another round with those gold shields!"

"Those guys are the stuff nightmares are made of. It's going to work out, Mark. I feel it."

Myra moved her hand to touch her shoulder, her eyes lighting up like Christmas trees. She squared her shoulders as she drew in a deep breath and moved closer to the cell door, but still far enough away so Chai couldn't touch her through the bars.

"Welcome to Pinewood, John Chai. This will be your home away from home into eternity. I'm Myra Rutledge. You killed my daughter and the child she carried. I've waited a very long time to meet you. Don't say a word in your defense, Mr. Chai, because if you do, I will have to close your lips permanently. I want you to take a good look at me and know you took away my child. There's nothing you can ever do to make it right. What that means to you, Mr. Chai, is this: I'm going to punish you for your crime. I'm going to make you wish you were dead. I am going to do terrible, unspeakable things to you. Even that won't be enough. Start praying, Mr. Chai." Without another word, Myra turned and started to walk away, the others following her.

Charles stayed behind a few more minutes. He pitched the bottle of water through the iron bars, along with the slice of stale bread. Chai's hysterical voice followed him all the way down the tunnel. He didn't look back.

Before Charles followed the women into the house he took a long moment to ponder what had just transpired. For some reason he'd expected Myra to get hysterical, to vent and wail. But she'd done none of those things. He wondered why.

In the kitchen the women resumed their preparations for their Thanksgiving dinner. They were talking about everything but John Chai. Charles noticed, however, that they watched Myra covertly. Myra was humming under her breath as she got dishes and mixing bowls out of the cabinets and placed them strategically along the counters. He couldn't help but wonder what was going to go into them. It was a wise man who knew when to retreat. Besides, he wanted to check with his friend Su Zhou Li to see what, if anything, was happening in his corner of the world. Charles excused himself and made his way to the war room. The women waved airily and continued with what they were doing.

An hour later a mantle of worry settled

over Charles's shoulders. Li wasn't answering either his house phone or the encrypted cell phones. He then tried his BlackBerry with the same result. He placed calls to old friends on the other side of the pond to see if they could find out any news on his old friend. Forty minutes later all his calls were returned with the same information. There was no trace of his old friend Su Zhou Li.

Charles looked down at his watch. Julia should be arriving any second now. He closed up shop, turned off the television monitors and set his machines to take all incoming messages. It was time to follow through on John Chai's visit.

In the kitchen, which was so fragrant he couldn't believe it, he headed straight for the circle of women to welcome Julia. She looked up, a radiant smile on her face.

"Charles!" She ran to him and gave him the biggest hug he'd ever had. "I feel like I finally came home! Oh, I missed you all so much. Yes, yes, I feel wonderful! Look at me, I put on ten pounds. My counts are all good. The doctors are more than pleased. Tell me I can do something now that I'm here. I'm not the least bit tired because I slept all the way here."

"If you think you're up to a little mission, we have one planned for you," Charles said, motioning to the others to gather round and listen. "Alexis will strip off your present disguise and give you a new one. You are going to become Mr. Gan Jun and you will be going to the Chinese embassy in Washington. Once inside, you will ask to use the rest room, get rid of the disguise, and leave with a second disguise that Alexis will provide you with. The plan is this. Everyone here will leave in their respective vehicles. If anyone is out there watching, and we have to assume they are, they can't follow all of you. I've taken the time to map out routes for each of you. When Julia leaves the embassy in her second disguise, she will be walking. One of you will pick her up and bring her back here in yet a third disguise. The rest of you will return here at different times during the evening. Go along, girls; Myra and I will finish up here. Lovely bird," he said, looking at the turkey sitting on the counter.

It was four o'clock when Charles wrapped the turkey in a damp towel and placed it in the refrigerator. He looked up, his jaw dropping. "Good Lord! Julia, you look more like Gan Jun than he did when he came in here. Good work, Alexis! Julia, remember, you're a mute. This is the paper you hand to the receptionist that simply says you are looking for your granddaughter who came to this country two years ago. Just bob your head up and down when they speak with you and get to the rest room as quickly as possible. Here is a map I lifted off the Internet showing the floor plan of the embassy. Are you sure you're up for this, my dear?"

"Charles, I am so up for this you cannot believe it. Don't worry, I can do it. Listen, I'd like a BLT when I get back, with some good American coffee."

"I'll see to it, my dear. All right now, everyone out at the same time. Good luck! Isabelle, you will be driving my Mercedes. Nikki will be driving Julia. Alexis will drive her own Mini Cooper and Kathryn will of course be driving her truck with Murphy. Myra is going to follow in her own Mercedes, which looks just like mine. Hurry now. If you encounter any problems, call me immediately."

Myra was the last to leave. Charles put a hand on her shoulder. "Are you . . . ?"

"Charles, I'm fine. I really am." She lowered her voice to a soft whisper. "Barbara . . . Barbara was . . . She talked to me,

Charles. That's how I was able to . . . to deal with John Chai. Oh, I have so much to tell you, but it will have to wait until tonight. We'll snuggle by the fireplace after the others go to bed. I have to go now; the girls are waiting for me. Love you."

Charles beamed with pleasure. "I'll be waiting, Myra."

Nikki and Julia kept up a running conversation about skiing in Switzerland, which neither one of them had ever done, the weather in general and Julia's hearty plant in Myra's kitchen. They were almost to Connecticut Avenue when Julia asked if there was any news of her husband, the former Senator Mitch Webster.

"You probably know as much as I do, Julia. Charles doesn't talk about it to any of us. He might discuss it with Myra, but I'm not sure. You know his rule: once a mission is over, it's over. We move on and don't discuss it. Do you care, Julia?"

"No, I don't care. I just want to know he's suffering."

Nikki laughed. "Working on a farm for twenty-five cents a week in Africa! I'd say he's suffering. It's a far cry from the Senate halls. But let's not talk about your ex-husband."

"He's not my ex, Nikki. We're still married. Charles is working on that end of it."

"We all missed you, Julia. You're coming back for Christmas, right?"

"Absolutely. I wouldn't miss Christmas at the farm for anything. I've been shopping like crazy. I'm doing so well, Nikki, it's scary. I know it's all experimental, but all cures start out that way. I'm very optimistic."

"I'm so glad, so happy for you, Julia. Look, we're almost there. Do you have it all straight? You're sure you can do this?"

"I'm sure, Nikki. This is some disguise. I really feel like an old Chinese man. I have my other clothes underneath. I go out the rear door next to a sitting room that is painted scarlet with gold accents. I can walk in either direction. I get in the first car I see that belongs to us. That's when I get rid of the second disguise, turn the jacket inside out, put on a new wig, gloves, muffler and hat. I replace my shoes with fur boots. I got it, Nikki. I have my paper that I give to the receptionist. I do have a question, though. If someone is following us — me in particular — what's to stop them from going into the embassy to ask where I am and what I'm doing there?"

"And you really think the receptionist

will talk with that person? Not in this life-time. That's a dead end for whoever is following you — if anyone is. OK, here we are, four-eight-four-nine Connecticut Ave. I'll double-park, get out, help you out and walk you to the door. Then I'll leave. You have your cell phone. Call any of us if there's a problem. Remember, walk stooped over, look like you're going to collapse any minute. Stop every few steps like you're trying to get your breathing under control."

"In my other life, my secret life I never talk about, I always wanted to be an actress, just like Alexis did."

"Be sure you give an Academy Award performance. Sit tight." Nikki stopped the car, got out and ran around to the passenger door and opened it. She wasted a few minutes, in case anyone was watching, to help Julia out of the car. Together they hobbled up to the entrance of the embassy. The door was opened almost immediately. Nikki stepped back when Julia handed the note to the two gentlemen standing on each side of the open door. They nodded and ushered Julia inside, at which point Nikki walked back to her car and drove away. She called Charles immediately.

"She's inside and I'm outta here. I didn't

spot a tail but that doesn't mean one isn't out there. See you in an hour. No traffic tonight. Guess everyone left the city for the long holiday weekend. See ya when I see ya."

Thirteen

Jack Emery swatted at his forehead not once but three times as he tried to comprehend what he was hearing. Conover had called to say all the women of Pinewood were leaving in separate vehicles.

"The old guy managed to walk out under his own power and he's getting into one of the cars. I can't get a good fix on it, Jack. Most of the cars are black and there are no lights on outside. The cars aren't putting their headlights on, either. Martin is still inside. The house is all lit up, smoke coming out of all the chimneys."

"Which car is the old gent in?"

"He was in the first one, I think, but they started to jockey the cars so the big rig could get turned around. Maybe the third one, then again it could be the second one. I can't see, Jack. These night-vision lenses are shit for the birds. What do you want me to do?"

"Nothing. Sit there and don't move."

The cell phone rang the moment Jack broke the connection with Conover. "You on it, Moody?"

"Yeah. Which one do you want me to follow?"

"Whichever car has two people in it."

"Jack, they aren't all going in the same direction. I can't see who's in the cars. And there's a cop sitting a half-mile up the road with a radar trap. Make up your mind, Jack, the cars are going past me right now."

"Where's the big rig?"

"It's in the lead. Then a sedan, a little Mini Cooper, then another sedan. Two cars split off and went in the other direction. There's one sitting on the road waiting for a break in traffic. Don't know which way she's going."

"That's only six cars. I thought there were seven."

"Six, Jack. Conover said the Asian girl hasn't come back. Six. What do you want me to do?"

"Follow the rig. I think they use it for . . . their tricks."

"OK. I can keep that one in sight. The other one just passed me. I got a good look at her because she's going slow. Older woman, gray hair, I think. She's wearing glasses."

"Stay with the rig, Moody. Report in as soon as you know something."

"OK, I'm outta here."

Jack slumped back in his chair. He looked at Mark through narrowed eyes. "They are smart!" He related the two phone calls for Mark's benefit.

"Maybe they're taking the old guy to the hospital or maybe they're taking him to a doctor who doesn't make house calls. It is a holiday weekend. If the old guy is sick they probably realize they aren't going to get a doctor easily if something is wrong. By the way, who was the old lady who arrived this afternoon?"

Jack shrugged. "No idea. Maybe a relative of Myra Rutledge's. The way Moody described her, it sounded like the old lady that was out at Pinewood a few months ago. Why are you asking?" Jack asked.

"No reason. Old lady, old guy, that kind of thing. Whoever she is, she's back at Pinewood with Martin. Don't suppose it means anything. It is Thanksgiving and people tend to invite other people for dinner. By the way, are you going to see your mother tomorrow?"

Jack rubbed at his temples. "I was going to but . . . Oh, she doesn't know me. I take her things and she gives them away. Once in a great while she'll call me Jackie like she remembers me, and then whatever was there is gone. I bawl my eyes out all the way home. I call almost every day. The nurses say she's happy in her own little world. She even has friends. She was taking piano lessons a few months ago. The amazing thing is she didn't forget from lesson to lesson. Go figure that one."

"I can't. I only asked in case you wanted me to go with you."

"I'll go for Christmas. Mom always loved Christmas. She'd start shopping in July and hide the stuff so my sister and I wouldn't find it. We always did. Man, did she decorate the house. It looked like the North Pole, Macy's and FAO Schwarz all rolled into one. My dad just humored her. She cooked for days and days, then gave half of it away. Sometimes I wish I was a kid again," Jack said, his voice cracking with emotion.

"Yeah, mothers are like that. I think we should pack up and go home, Jack."

"Yeah, let's go home."

Mark clapped his friend on the back. "We're going to get to the bottom of this one way or the other. They might be smart, Jack, but they aren't *that* smart.

Sooner or later one of them is going to mess up. That's when we'll get them."

Mark turned off the lights and locked the door. A light snow was falling as they made their way to their cars.

Jack climbed behind the wheel of his car. Half his mind was on his mother and the other half was thinking about what Mark had said about old people.

In the restroom Julia entered one of the stalls and removed the two-piece black sack suit with the assorted padding. She stuffed it into the trash bin. Underneath, she wore bright-red slacks with a matching sweater jacket. She ripped at the gray wig, the mustache and the goatee, folded all three into a tight square, and stuffed it into the pocket of her sweater. She was now wearing a short black wig. The black fur boots looked fashionable and had been covered by the baggy black pants. The last thing she did was take a little ball of latex from her pocket. She positioned a bit of it at the corner of each eye. She immediately took on an Asian appearance.

Julia exited the stall, looked around to be sure no one was watching her. She opened the door cautiously and peered out. No one was in sight. She walked out boldly, looking neither to the right nor the left. In less than three minutes she was outside, walking down a path that took her around to the front of the embassy on Connecticut Avenue. She turned right and started to walk briskly. She saw the Mini Cooper coming toward her. Within seconds, she was across the street and in the car. Alexis shifted gears and peeled down the road.

"How'd it go?" she asked, anxiety ringing in her voice.

"Piece of cake, baby, piece of cake. I really didn't see anyone except the receptionist and those two guys who let me in. By the way, they keep the door locked at all times. This is just a guess on my part, but I think they're operating with just a skeleton crew."

Traffic was light as Alexis drove down Connecticut Avenue. The roads were wet and slick with the falling snow. "Call Charles so he can let the others know we're on our way back, then shed that outfit. Your new duds are on the back seat."

Julia looked over her shoulder. She started to laugh when she saw the snow-white Stetson. "Damn, you are good. How'd you know I always wanted to be a cowgirl?"

"You told me once if you couldn't be an actress you wanted to be a cowgirl. I took that into consideration."

"I was ten years old when those desires were the most important thing in the world to me. Look at me now, I'm a doctor who can't practice my profession because my husband gave me AIDS. I'm fighting for my life by undergoing experimental treatment in Switzerland. Don't think I'm complaining, Alexis. I'm just grateful I'm alive."

"And you're going to stay that way for a very long time. Hey, did you see how well your plant is doing? We all literally hover over it and breathe on it. It's thriving, just like you are."

"Thanks," was all Julia could say as she struggled to dress herself in the new outfit. This time she would be wearing jeans, plaid shirt, denim jacket, cowboy boots, a blonde wig with a ponytail and the white Stetson.

"Home, James!" she giggled.

Alexis smiled. It was good to see and hear the old Julia. "You got it, Miss Cowgirl!"

Charles looked around the war room. Even though it was almost midnight, the women looked wired. Especially Myra and Julia. He wasn't sure if it was a good or bad thing. He stepped down and away from the bank of computers where he'd been working. "Let's talk, ladies. We need to decide on Mr. Chai's punishment."

Myra looked up at the women she now viewed as daughters. She smiled at them and said only one word. "Caning."

"You mean like they do in Asia? Whipping him?" Isabelle asked.

Myra nodded. "Yes. It may be barbaric, but they still do it. Over there, it is acceptable. Over here, they'd probably lynch us from a tree if we tried something like that. But, since no one knows what we're about, I think it's a just punishment. Tell me what you think."

"Hey, if it floats your boat, Myra, I'm all for it," Kathryn said. "I'll flick the bamboo pole myself if that's what you want." The others nodded in agreement.

"Then what?" Nikki asked.

Myra looked puzzled at the question. "What do you mean?"

Nikki spoke. "After we cane him, then what? We agreed not to kill him. That leaves the question of what to do with him. Do we send him back to China, or another country, or do we keep him here in the tunnels until he rots? We could probably drive him insane if we played rap music twenty-four-seven along with shining a bunch of Maglites into his cell. That's what they did with Noriega. It's whatever you want, Myra."

"I don't know, dear, I didn't get that far in my thinking. I thought we'd leave him alone tomorrow since it's Thanksgiving. Then on Friday we could begin. I am of course open to any and all suggestions."

Kathryn grimaced. "I'd like to shove a pair of chopsticks up his ass and send him off to fend for himself when we're done with him."

"Yeah," Alexis said. "Just so the chopsticks are full of splinters." The women laughed. Charles flinched.

"What do you think, Charles? Should we think about sending him back to China or should we . . . make arrangements here at home for . . . our guest?"

"At this point in time, Myra, I really don't have an opinion, much less an answer. I haven't been able to reach Su Zhou Li. I don't want to put him in any more danger by asking him to help us again. We pushed the envelope the first time around. So, for the moment, Mr. Chai will have to be our guest. Shall we go to the tunnels and bid him goodnight?"

"That's a splendid idea. After we do that, shall we start with the bright lights and the rap music? We'll need a few moments to gather up a few things to take with us. Girls, come with me," Myra said.

Charles waited, tapping his foot and kneading his hands together. He couldn't even begin to imagine what the women were gathering up inside the house. He gawked, stepping backward as they entered the war room dressed in hooded black cloaks. Each of them had their arms full of bags.

"We're ready, dear," Myra said.

Charles led the parade out of the war room and down the steps that would take them to the tunnels and John Chai. Charles reached for one of the Maglites that Nikki was carrying. He stuck it up on the wall next to the other light. The blinding white lights shone directly into John Chai's cell. The women set the gear they were holding on the ground before they formed a straight line in front of the cell. John Chai looked at them, fear shining in his eyes.

"What are you going to do?" he screamed. "Let me out of this hellhole! My father will find you and kill you if you harm me in any way."

"No, your father won't find us. He won't find you, either," Julia said quietly. The words were said with such quiet authority that Chai backed up until his legs hit the metal bed.

Chai started to stutter. "It was an accident. I didn't mean for it to happen."

Myra's voice was just as quiet and commanding as Julia's had been. "You were drinking. You were driving too fast. You didn't stop; you left the scene of the accident and then you left the country," she said. "You have to pay for your cowardice."

"Money! My father is very wealthy. I am wealthy. How much money do you want? What are you going to do to me? This is barbaric!"

"Barbaric? You ain't seen nothing yet, Mister Chai!" Kathryn said.

"Who are you?" Chai snarled.

Nikki stepped forward. She knew the hooded black robes frightened the man behind the bars. "We're your judges. We're your jury. We're your —"

A string of venomous Chinese words ricocheted off the earthen walls. The women looked at Charles for a translation.

"You don't want to know what he said.

This might be a good time to tell our guest what he has to look forward to."

Myra walked over to the cell and reached for the bars in both hands. "Tomorrow is a holiday for us. Thanksgiving. Nothing will happen to you until the following day, when we all come back down here. You will be caned, Mr. Chai."

Chai leaped forward just as Charles drew Myra away from the cell.

"That's inhuman!" Chai snarled.

"Tell that to your people who do it on a daily basis to prisoners in your country. When asked about it, your father said he approved of the punishment. I can show you the actual interview where your father made that statement. Enough time, it's late and tomorrow is a holiday. We need to get some rest, as do you, Mr. Chai," Charles said.

The women got busy. The large clock from Myra's kitchen was hooked on to the bottom of the Maglite. Nikki set up a folding table while Isabelle put bowls of food on it. Alexis checked the CD player and the long-playing rap disc. She cranked it as loud as it would go. Myra hung up thick quilts on the pegs jutting out from the wall. Everything was out of John Chai's reach.

"We'll be back in exactly thirty-one hours," Nikki shouted. "Count the minutes and the seconds, you son of a bitch!"

"You can't do this! What kind of people are you? I told you, it was an accident! You have no right to take the law into your own hands. You have no right!"

Kathryn ran back to the cell. "No right? No right! Listen, you slimy bastard, we have every right in the world! You killed Barbara Rutledge. Women brought you to this point, so you just think about that when you try to sleep tonight — you just think about that! By the way, the rats down here are very skinny. We aren't behind those bars begging for our life, you are. And to think you were brought down by a bunch of women. Oh, well, you won't have any face left to save when we're done with you."

The women clapped their hands in approval.

"Girls, don't you think it was clever of me to stop at the costume shop for these hooded robes while we were all driving around Washington? The young man looked at me so strangely when I bought those rap CDs at the music store. I said I was having a party. I don't think he believed me. That man is worse than I thought. He won't freeze down there, will he, Charles?" Myra asked.

"He has a blanket. He'll be so busy watching the rats eat all the food you left on the table that he won't be able to sleep. Of course, eventually he will sleep. Good-night, ladies. I still have some work to do."

"But, Charles . . ." Myra said.

"Forty minutes, that's all, Myra. I'll join you by the fire. Will you wait for me?"

Myra stopped, turned around and walked back to where Charles was stand-ing. "You don't ever have to ask me a ques-tion like that. I will wait for you forever. Don't you know you are the light of my life, the wind beneath my sails? Maybe we should forgo the wine and the fire and get right to the *good stuff.*"

Charles laughed. "Now, that's an offer I wouldn't even think of refusing. You're on, old girl!"

Myra giggled all the way into the house. The girls watched her as she giggled her way to the second floor. Then they grinned and winked at one another.

"I think Myra has more sex than all of us put together," Kathryn grumbled. "We all have to stop waiting for the White Knight to find us. We need to start *searching* for him. Actively. *Really* actively."

"And when they want to know what we *do*, assuming we find someone who is enamored with us, what do we say?" Isabelle asked.

"You're raining on my parade, Isabelle. Night, everyone," Kathryn grumbled again.

"Night," said the others.

Fourteen

The women of Pinewood clustered around the back door and kitchen window to admire the winter wonderland. Eight inches of new snow covered the rolling hills of Myra's estate. "It's beautiful!" they said as one.

Myra looked up at Charles. "Should we tell them now?" she whispered.

"I can see you are chomping at the bit to tell. I thought you said you could keep a secret," Charles teased.

Myra leaned into Charles. "That was then; this is now. All that glorious whiteness might be gone by Christmas and then the presents will be worthless. They'll just sit in the barn."

"Then, my dear, by all means tell them."

"Girls! Girls! Charles and I want to give you all an early Christmas present. After breakfast, of course. Snowmobiles! One for each of you! Kathryn's has a side seat for Murphy!"

They were like children again as they whooped and hollered, high-fived and hugged.

It was the ever practical Yoko who said, "But Mr. Chai's thirty-one hours are about up. Are we delaying his punishment or do we frolic afterward?"

Myra looked at Charles. She shrugged. "Mr. Chai can wait a little longer. I can wait a little longer. Charles has cooked a magnificent breakfast for all of you. Kippers and sausage — and don't ask me where he got the kippers. The man is a total mystery to me at times. We have crispy bacon, eggs Benedict, banana and macadamia nut pancakes with maple syrup, and all the coffee and juice we can drink."

"You dear, sweet man," Kathryn said as she snatched two pieces of bacon, one for her and one for Murphy. "Are the snow-mobiles primed and gassed?"

"Charles did it all before he left for China. When you get back from your play-time, we'll have hot chocolate with those little marshmallows and ginger cookies waiting. Nikki and Barbara always looked forward to that little treat when they came in from sledding."

Nikki smiled. "All we did was think

about the marshmallows while we were out in the snow. Myra," she explained, "was a stickler about our teeth and sweets, so marshmallows were a real treat. There was never any candy in the house either. Try and figure that one out." She knew in her gut that there would be one extra snowmobile in the old barn. For Barbara. A machine that would stay bright and shiny forever. She also knew it would be sunshine yellow, Barbara's favorite color.

Myra beamed as she threw her hands in the air. "You see, I never knew that. Oh, well!"

Charles served breakfast and the women gobbled their food so they could go outdoors to play in the snow.

"Julia . . ."

"I'm fine, Myra. I'm up for it. I have to confess, I never drove a snowmobile, but I'm willing to learn. It can't be half as hard as those motorcycles we all drove on Kathryn's mission. I'm excited. I want my hot chocolate *loaded* with marshmallows!"

"I'll personally take care of it. Run along, girls. Charles and I will clean up here. Then we'll see to Mr. Chai's comfort. Not that we really care about his comfort. It's just something Charles and I will do to look busy. Isn't that right, dear?"

Charles just laughed as he stacked the dishwasher.

"Dress warmly, girls, especially you, Julia," Myra said in a motherly tone. "Have fun but don't stay out too long."

The girls barreled out the door like children and raced to the barn. Within minutes all Charles and Myra could hear was shrill laughter and the high-pitched whine of the snowmobiles.

Myra looked down at her watch. "I have this insane urge to speak with Mr. Chai. Oh, dear, put *more* food on that platter. A little of everything. There are so many rats down there. What are we giving Mr. Chai?"

Charles looked around at the bright kitchen. "Something nourishing, I think. Maybe a few slices of banana and a piece of bread. Half a bottle of water."

"Excellent, Charles! A pretty dish, but not one of my heirlooms. I think the pink one from the Pottery Barn. I can always order more. You don't think he froze to death during the night, do you, Charles?" She said this last as though she was discussing the weather.

"I doubt it. The man is too mean to die. We did give him *one* blanket. I'm ready, Myra."

Carrying the pink dish, Myra led the way

down through the tunnels. She reached up twice to ring the bells, but knew Chai wouldn't be able to hear them with the rap music blasting all along the tunnels. She shuddered at the horrible sound.

The moment John Chai saw Myra and Charles, he rushed to the iron bars and screamed at the top of his lungs. "Let me out of here, you bastards!"

Charles calmly reached up to turn off the CD player.

"Good morning, Mr. Chai. Name-calling is not a nice thing. Oh, look, dear, the food is all gone. No matter, we brought more," Myra said.

"I'm freezing! My feet are blue! I'm starving! That goddamn light is blinding me! I can barely hear. You're inhuman. Damn you, let me out of here!"

"Do you really want to get into a discussion on human rights, Mr. Chai? You need to be quiet. We just came down here to tell you that your punishment has been delayed a few hours. We could give you another blanket, I suppose. What do you think, dear?" Myra asked.

Charles shrugged. "We could."

"But we won't," Myra said. "If you step away from the bars, Mr. Chai, I'll give you some food. If you don't move, it stays right here for your other roommates. By the way, they're going to feast on kippers, sausages, bacon, banana-macadamia nut pancakes with warm butter and syrup, plus eggs Benedict. Doesn't that sound scrumptious? Oh dear, the man simply doesn't follow instructions." Without another word or glance, Myra let the pink dish fall to the ground. "I have to leave now, Mr. Chai, but I'll be back."

Charles turned on the CD player again. Myra walked over to the cell but stood away from the bars. "I spent years hating you. Until the day before yesterday, I didn't have a face to match to that hatred. My hatred hasn't lessened now that I've seen you. In fact, my hatred has increased. By the way, no one in your country is looking for you. Tomorrow we will have some newspapers to prove it. I'm sorry you didn't want any breakfast."

"Stop with the lies! My father will have the government, the military and all his people looking for me. He will leave no stone unturned until I am home safe and sound. That man Li is already dead, I can promise you that."

Charles turned off the CD player again. The sudden silence was deafening. He spoke quietly but distinctly. "You should never make a promise you can't possibly keep, Mr. Chai. No one is looking for you. No one. Mr. Li is safely out of your country. I spoke with him earlier and he is probably sitting down to an early luncheon — in another country, of course," Charles lied with a straight face. "You are not important enough, even to your own father, to warrant such a search. You're what we call a bad penny, a disgrace to your family. No one cares about you, Mr. Chai, so get used to the idea. We're all you have going for you at the moment. Now, if you'll excuse me, I have to think about what I'm going to serve for our own lunch." He reached up to turn the CD player to full volume. Chai's curses followed him all the way back to the mouth of the tunnel. Just for fun, he rang the cluster of rusty bells. The merry sound stayed with him all the way up the steps that led to the ground floor of the farmhouse.

Jack Emery woke to the shrill ringing of the phone in the apartment. Bleary-eyed and disgruntled, he made his way to the living room, picked up the phone and barked a greeting. He listened as he padded his way to the window where he gasped in surprise.

"OK, OK, I heard you the first time, Moody. Yeah, yeah, I understand Conover can't do his surveillance with the snowplows out. I said you could go home, what the hell is your problem, Moody?" Jack listened, his eyes murderous as the operative continued. "I know about footprints in the snow. You're right, Moody. Either Mark or I will be in touch."

Jack stalked his way to the kitchen where Mark was making coffee and toast. "Well, even the weatherman is against us. He didn't say one word about that goddamn snow out there. He said *flurries*. Does that look like flurries to you?"

Mark spread butter on the toast when it popped up. "Looks to me like about eight to ten inches. That means we have to shovel out our cars. Listen, Jack, even you can't expect some dumbass dick to sit in a tree with all that snow. Get real here. As for Conover, give that up, too. The plows will move all that snow to the side of the road and there's no place to park there, even if it is a country road. We need to fall back and regroup. Want some toast?"

Jack reached for the toast Mark held out. He chomped down, his guts churning and twisting. "Son of a fucking bitch! I thought you said you made coffee!"

Mark handed over a cup of black coffee. Jack gulped at it. "You got any big, like really big, pieces of paper? I'm going to make a chart and put every *squirrely* little detail down. A map of sorts. I always did that at the DA's office. When you see something in black and white it makes a difference. So, you got any paper?"

"Only copy paper. Tape them together. You can do that while I take a shower. I used to do the same thing at the Bureau back at the beginning. The other fibbies used to laugh at me but I solved two cases with those maps and it was from the little details that no one else thought about. Good thinking, Jack. Let's not worry about shoveling till later. There are some teenagers who live in this complex. They might come around looking for money to shovel." Mark looked around but Jack was already gone. Talk about a man with tunnel vision, a one-track mind, a dog with a bone. Jack was that man.

The women entered the kitchen rosy-cheeked and laughing. They were all covered with snow. Myra ushered them into the laundry room, where they shed their outer gear.

Myra smiled as Julia hugged her.

"Thank you for that, Myra. I don't know when I've ever had so much fun." She grinned and said, "Well, maybe that day we learned to ride those motorcycles. That was *fun!* You should have seen Murphy chasing us all. He didn't want to sit in his seat except when it was time to come in. Now, where's that hot chocolate and all those marshmallows?"

Charles filled oversize soup cups with the creamy hot chocolate, the marshmallows melting into a gooey white mess on top. They all laughed at their sticky white mustaches as they regaled Myra and Charles with describing their childish escapade in the snow.

And then it was over and time to descend the stone steps to the tunnels. The laughter and camaraderie was left behind in the kitchen as they once again donned the black hooded robes. It was now time to do what they'd come here to do: time to exact Myra's vengeance for the killing of her daughter.

Nothing in the cell block of the tunnel had changed since Myra and Charles's earlier visit. The rap music was still reverberating along the walls. The food on the platter was seriously depleted. John Chai was still screaming, hoarse now with the effort.

Kathryn walked over to the cell. "Shut up. No one is interested in anything you have to say. Keep it up, and when it's my turn with the bamboo cane, you'll wish you had listened."

John Chai moved as far back in the cell as he could go. Fear and hatred shone from his eyes, but he was not above a little begging. He dropped to his knees, his hands outstretched. "Don't do this! I'll give you anything you want. I'll do anything you want me to do. Caning is . . . Please don't do that to me."

"You're whining, Chinese boy. I have to tell you, it is not manly, nor is it becoming from someone of your family's prominence," Nikki snarled. "C'mon now, be a man and step forward. Or we'll come in there and drag you out. We'll be taking pictures as we do it. How's that going to look back in China? You'll be a joke to your people."

Chai looked from one woman to the other, hoping to see some reluctance on their part. All he could see past the hooded robes was stony confirmation that nothing he said would sway their decision to cane him within an inch of his life. If there had been anything in his stomach he would have retched at the sight of the bamboo cane that would take the skin right off his body. He started to shake as he cried and begged to deaf ears.

Charles unlocked the heavy iron door. Kathryn and Nikki walked into the cell. Chai bounced up, literally leaping in the air, his legs kicking out in both directions, knocking both Kathryn and Nikki to the ground. With his arms straight out in front of him, he charged through the open cell door and used the fingers of his right hand to jab Myra in the throat in a lightning-quick motion while his left hand, fingers stiff as rods, stabbed at Charles's nose. Alexis squealed as she threw the platter of food at him, while Julia ducked around and ran to Nikki and Kathryn, who were struggling to their feet. Yoko stripped off her robe and dropped to a crouch, her arms positioned the same as Chai's.

Yoko's voice took on a sing-song lilt. "Let's see how good you are, Mr. Chai. I know every move you know and then some. You learned your art to intimidate people. I learned mine to *kill*."

Charles, his eyes wide with horror, did his best to mop at the blood gushing from his nose, which he knew was broken, as Myra struggled to breathe. He prayed that Chai hadn't crushed her larynx.

"Are you perhaps waiting for a bus, Mr. Chai?" Yoko sing-songed. In the blink of an eye she was off the ground, twirling this way and that, her legs outstretched like those of a gymnast. Chai moved but still took the brunt of her foot in the middle of his stomach. He went down but was back on his feet in the time it took to take a breath, his own feet and hands lashing out. Yoko danced away, then, quicker than lightning, moved forward to jab Chai deep in the throat. He gagged, doubled over, but remained on his feet. She lashed out with her foot and then hooked him behind the knee. He went down and she was on his back, the collar of his shirt in both her hands. Without breaking a sweat, she bent his head forward and banged it against the earthen floor until he passed out.

"Where in the damn hell did you learn to do *that?*" Kathryn gasped as she clutched at her tender stomach.

"From my aunts, the women who raised me. We learn this art as soon as we can walk. It is mandatory. I excelled," she said proudly. "I think we should tie him up now. To that beam over there. Is everyone all right?"

Myra looked around at the girls. "I'm

fine. What I mean is, I will be fine. Charles, is your nose broken?"

"I'm afraid so, dear. I can't believe . . . I was asleep at the switch. I'm beyond embarrassed. Let's get Mr. Chai trussed up before he tries another go at us. Excellent work, Yoko. One day you will teach me some of those movements. Absolutely wonderful."

Yoko tried to look demure but she was having too good a time. "It will be my pleasure, Charles."

Myra looked from one to the other. "I think we should go upstairs for some tea. Tea always makes things better, don't you agree, girls? We need to get Charles to a doctor."

"Myra, there's nothing they can do for a broken nose. Julia is here. She can do whatever has to be done. Besides, how would a doctor get out here in all this snow? Tea is a wonderful idea. Are you sure you're all right, my dear?"

"Charles, I will survive. Come along, girls, we're going upstairs for tea. Mr. Chai can wait. We have the rest of *his* life."

Fifteen

Jack Emery pushed away from his desk and did his best to work the kinks out of his neck and shoulders. Sitting across from him, Mark did the same thing.

"We've been at this for eight solid hours, Jack. I gave you my input; what are you putting on the table, if anything?"

Jack rubbed at his temples. He had a throbbing headache that seemed to be getting worse by the hour. Maybe he needed glasses. He made a mental note to schedule an eye doctor appointment. He pointed to the sloppy-looking map he'd taped to the wall across from where he and Mark were sitting. "Every stinking, miserable detail is up there. It goes all the way back to the day Barbara Rutledge was killed. I didn't leave a thing out. It's all there, but I'm missing something. It's there, Mark, right in front of us. What am I missing?"

The ex-FBI agent shrugged. "I don't

know, Jack. I'm seeing what you're seeing. I agree we're missing something here, but what is it?"

"The unlikely group of women. What's that all about? I don't know why but I think Nikki is the one who brought them all together. The black girl is an ex-con. Ask yourself why Myra would socialize with an ex-con. Her defense was that she was falsely accused. The Asian girl is another question. My background check on her didn't bring up anything significant, so she remains a question mark. Myra has a gardener who now all of a sudden is helping out at the Asian girl's nursery. I find that a little weird but explainable as there isn't much for a gardener to do in the winter. Then there's the architect who has been living at the poverty level since she was found guilty of vehicular homicide. She lost everything — her license, her home, her business. It could be that Myra feels sorry for her and, at Nikki's request, is helping her. She did do some work at Pinewood last year. Her claim is she wasn't driving the car the day of the accident. Falsely accused.

"Which brings us to Dr. Julia Webster. She's a real mystery in more ways than one. She resigned, retired, whatever, from her position at the hospital, supposedly to help her senator husband campaign for the Vice Presidency. Scandal erupts, then Senator Webster and Dr. Webster suddenly disappear off the face of the earth. They disappeared just the way Marie Lewellen and her family disappeared. Solid brick wall there.

"Then we have the chick with the eighteen-wheeler. I hauled her ass into my office last year and Nikki was her lawyer. Think about that truck, Mark. She and her truck-driver buddies shut down the Interstate when the troopers tried to pull her in. In the end, she came willingly. Rock-solid alibi on the Lewellen snatch. She had an answer for everything. Nikki went to the wall for her. That's what I mean, she's tied to all these women somehow. Not just legally, either.

"And, of course, there's Myra and that pot of money she controls. And her guy Martin. We sure as hell know who he is and the connections he has." Jack bounded off his chair and walked around to the poster on the wall. With a red grease pencil he printed the words: *Lucas/18-wheeler, Martin/connections.* Underneath that he wrote: *Myra, pots of money* followed by: *ex-con/architect/falsely accused.* The last two names to be added with the red grease pencil were: *Nikki/exceptionally sharp lawyer/myra's adopted daughter/ Barbara's sister* and then: *Asian girl?*

"The question mark means she doesn't compute. Do you agree or disagree, Mark?"

"Well, yeah, I do. What could the Asian girl bring to this particular party? Plants, flowers, shrubs? What?"

Jack added another word: CHINESE. "The guy who killed Myra's daughter was a Chinese diplomat's son with diplomatic immunity. They whisked him out of the country in less than twenty-four hours. If he comes back here, it is my understanding that he can be arrested and prosecuted. He ain't coming back, Mark. At least not willingly."

Mark's eyes popped. "Martin, Nikki, the Asian girl and the ex-con flew to China for four or five days. They brought back a guest, an old guy who looked frail and sick."

Jack stomped his foot. "Key word here, Mark. *Looked* old and frail." The grease pencil squealed on the paper as Jack scribbled.

"Then an old lady shows up mid-afternoon. Old lady, old man. A switch? Why? What would be the purpose?"

215

"Keep that train of thought. Old lady arrives. Old guy leaves. Everyone at Pinewood except Charles left that night. In separate vehicles. Except . . . except for Nikki, who drove the old guy. What we don't know is where she took him. Think, Mark, where would she take him? A hospital? But you checked the database at all the local hospitals and no one matching his description was admitted that night. Clinics do not keep overnight patients. A relative? Possible, but doubtful. They returned in less than three hours so they couldn't have gone too far. The ex-con picked up another guest, a woman who looked like a cowgirl, complete with Stetson and boots. Nikki dropped off the old guy somewhere and the ex-con picks up a cowgirl. How do we explain the cowgirl?"

Mark started to pace. "Whatever it is, they planned it. Hey, Jack, did you ever consider the Chinese embassy? There's three of them. Two are on Connecticut Avenue. I don't know offhand where the other one is. That would make sense. Martin brings the old guy here because he needs medical help. Who better to help him than his own people at the Chinese embassy? I gotta tell you, the cowgirl has me stumped. I don't think she's part of all this. More than likely she's a friend they invited for Thanksgiving. People do that, Jack, invite people who will be alone. That's what Thanksgiving is all about."

"Nah, those women don't do things like that. They're all meaner than snakes. The cowgirl is important somehow. We just have to figure out the why of it . . . Hey, all this thinking is making me thirsty — want a beer?"

"Yeah. Bring some *munchies.* I think better when I'm chewing."

Jack obliged, returning with two beers and a box of Ritz crackers.

"I'm just thinking out loud here, Mark. There were seven women when this all began. Then Dr. Webster disappears, leaving just six women. Then, the day before Thanksgiving, an old lady arrives, the old guy splits and a cowgirl shows up. The cowgirl makes seven women. Think, Mark!"

"Think what, Jack? Eight women if you count the old lady."

"You know what I think, Mark? I think the old guy is John Chai in disguise. I think the old lady is Dr. Webster, a.k.a. the cowgirl. They're using disguises. One of them has to be pretty damn good at it. Get out that file on the ex-con. Something is tickling me about her."

"Ah, shit, Jack, that's a stretch even for you," Mark said as he dutifully pulled up Alexis Thorne's profile on the computer. He printed it out.

Jack swiveled in his chair to reach for the printout. "Aha! Read it and weep, ye of little faith! Read it out loud, buddy, and I already accept your apology."

"Blah, blah, blah. Subject had acting aspirations but no talent. Intense interest in Little Theater. Volunteer makeup artist. Excelled in costume design. She had a mentor who taught her everything he knew. But volunteer work didn't pay, so with her degree in business she went to work for a small brokerage house and did quite well until she was arrested for securities fraud. She still volunteered nights and weekends at the Little Theater. It says here she travels with a red bag. A *big* red bag. That's in addition to her purse and a suitcase when she goes to Pinewood. Nikki Quinn is her attorney."

Jack thumped his beer bottle on the desk. "Do you still think I'm nuts? Let's come up with a story and call those three embassies. Depending on the information we get, if any, I'm going to call Nikki and arrange a meeting."

"Man, you do love living dangerously, don't you, Jack? A word of advice. Keep remembering those gold shields."

"Oh, yeah, how could I forget those gold shields? Start thinking, Mark. We need to come up with a sympathetic story for the Chinese."

Julia peeled off her latex gloves and tossed them in the trash. "You have to keep the ice pack on for as long as you can stand it. Ideally twenty minutes on, twenty minutes off. Since you refused to go to the hospital, I did the best I could. If that monster had used the palm of his hand to push your nose in up to your brain, you'd be dead, Charles. Be grateful, if you can, that your nose is just broken. I'll check the packing tomorrow. I have pain pills if you need them. For now, I'd take a couple of shots of whiskey. I know, I know, you want your wits about you. I just want you to know I have the pain pills if you need them."

"Thank you, Julia. I'm going to clean up and change my clothes. Make more tea, Myra." This last was said to give Myra something to do so she wouldn't blame herself for the incident in the tunnels.

"I'll do that, Charles. Tea is such a . . . a wonderful thing. Hot tea. Real tea. Sugar tea. I love tea. Charles loves tea. Everyone loves tea . . . I really don't feel like making tea," Myra said, sitting down with a thump. "That . . . that scurrilous man. We should break his legs, gouge his eyes out, pull out his tongue and . . . his toenails and finger-nails, too. He could have killed Charles and seriously hurt you girls. What kind of person is that man?"

Nikki's voice was soothing. "Charles is fine. We're all fine. We learned a lesson. And we're all grateful to Yoko. Don't worry about the tea. We're up to here," Nikki said, motioning to her throat, "with tea. You need to relax now or you won't be any good to us. We need you. Charles is fine. Are you listening to me, Myra?"

"Of course I'm listening. Thank you so much, girls. We do work well together, don't we?"

"We're the best," Kathryn said. She turned to Yoko. "Baby, you need to teach us how to do all that stuff you did down there. When you have time, that is."

"It will be my pleasure, Kathryn. Anyone can learn the movements. The real art is in cleansing your mind and being one with what you are doing. It is instinctive to a certain degree."

"I can do that," Kathryn said. "Well, I think I can do that. I don't know about the Buddhist part, though. The last time I looked, I was a Baptist."

"I will overlook that part," Yoko said and giggled.

Charles appeared in the doorway wearing a blue flannel shirt and khaki corduroy trousers. He looked madder than hell. The women sobered instantly as they rose to follow him to the tunnels.

Last in line, Nikki felt her cell phone vibrate in her pocket. She motioned the others to go ahead of her when she saw the number of the caller. *Jack Emery.* She retraced her steps to the kitchen and sat down.

"Hello, Jack."

"Hi, Nik. How are you?"

"I'm well. How about you? Do you miss the DA's office?"

"At times. I'm just one of those people who doesn't react well to coercion, cover-ups and the like. Anyway, that's not why I called you. I figured it out. All of it. I'm giving you the courtesy of this call before I blow the whistle on your little operation."

Nikki grew so light-headed she had to

hold on to the chair. "Jack, why are you doing this? You're obsessed. You need to give it up and get on with your life."

"Tell me if I'm wrong about this. You brought John Chai back here to the States. You had him right there at Pinewood. Dr. Webster was an old lady and then she was a cowgirl. How'm I doing so far, Nik?"

Nikki thought her heart was going to jump out of her chest. "Are you drunk, Jack?"

"No, Nik, I'm not drunk. You guys use Lucas and her rig. I know all about the black girl and her red bag. This is just a heads up, Nik. Do you want to meet?"

Nikki thought she was going to choke on her own saliva. Somehow, she managed to say, "OK, Jack, one more time. I'll meet you tomorrow morning at Mulligan's if you can afford breakfast. Eight o'clock."

"Good. Mulligan's at eight. I'm flush enough for donuts and coffee."

Nikki blinked when the line went dead. She shoved the cell phone back into her pocket. She was shaking so badly she had to bend over to take deep breaths before she raced to the tunnels. Right now she didn't have time to think about Jack and his threatening phone call. She'd think about all that later.

The rap music was turned off but the lights were still blinding. No one questioned Nikki about her phone call. The women had donned their hooded robes and Nikki slipped into hers, not fully understanding the significance, but thinking that if it was what Myra wanted then she would do it. Maybe they used black robes in China for this sort of thing. She was still so light-headed after Jack's phone call that she couldn't think straight. *How did Jack figure it all out? Was he guessing? Did he have proof? Would he really turn her and the others over to the authorities?*

"There you are, dear. Is everything all right? You look pale. Mr Chai is securely trussed up, so don't worry about him getting loose."

Nikki shivered inside the flimsy black robe. "I'm all right, Myra. How are you holding up?"

"Just fine, dear, now that I know Charles is all right. I did have a few bad moments there. I can't say I blame our guest for going berserk. Under the same circumstances, I would fight like a tiger. I think most people would. Mr. Chai seems to have accepted his present situation, at least for now. He looks quite docile, don't you think?"

"He's tied up, Myra, he really doesn't have any choice. If he moves or struggles, his bonds cut into his flesh."

"He's not quite as belligerent as he was before he threw his little . . . tantrum that we managed to squelch. He's such an . . . an unsavory person," Myra said, always the lady.

"He's a ring-tailed son of a bitch, Myra," Nikki said through her clenched teeth. *And Jack Emery knows all about him.*

Nikki drew Myra aside and whispered. "Did you and Charles decide what we're going to do with Chai once this is all over?"

"I'm not sure, dear. I think the plan is to drop him off at the Chinese embassy. That may have changed since we discussed it. We did discuss sending him to England. Personally, I don't much care where he goes or what he does once I get finished with him. Do you have any suggestions, Nikki?"

"If something comes to me, I'll let you know. Are you ready, Myra?"

"I'm ready, dear." Myra reached for the bamboo cane.

Sixteen

It was a ceremony of sorts. The seven women stepped aside so that Myra could go to the head of the line. Charles's expression was inscrutable, his hands rock steady. This was his vengeance as much as it was Myra's. Barbara was his daughter, too. It was his decision, not Myra's, to keep it a secret, even from Barbara, who had loved him dearly. After her death, he told himself, over and over, some things were better left alone. His daughter's death was one of those things.

Myra balanced the cane in her hand. It was heavier than she expected, which meant she would have to use both hands when it was time to strike the man standing in front of her. Holding the cane, she started the slow walk around the naked form of John Chai, the others close behind. Each of them took a minute to stare at the man they were going to cane. No one blinked; no one flinched.

John Chai begged with his eyes and then he sobbed as he pleaded for mercy. The women ignored him as they took up positions behind Myra. When Chai's sobs stopped, the silence was so total it was deafening.

The women expected Myra to make a short speech but she didn't. Instead she raised the cane and said, "You know why this is happening. Don't insult me again by begging." The cane found its mark in the middle of Chai's shoulders, the tails flinging to the right and left. Olive-colored skin flew in all directions. The cane came down a second time across Chai's buttocks, the tails striking him on his thighs. Blood and skin spurted outward. Chai squealed like a stuck pig. Myra lowered the cane and stepped forward to peer at the damage she'd done before she handed the cane to Kathryn.

Kathryn hefted the cane as though it was a javelin. She walked around to the front of the chair and, with the end of the cane, lifted his chin. "Look at me!" Chai squeezed his eyes shut. He whimpered like a sick cat. Kathryn backed up several steps, flexed the cane as she judged the distance and tried to figure out how much damage the tails could do. She backed up two more steps and in the blink of an eye the cane came down on Chai's mid-section. He squealed again and again, cursing in Chinese as he sagged under his bonds. The cane came up again and Kathryn brought it down across his groin, the bamboo tails splitting every inch of skin they came in contact with. Chai passed out as Kathryn handed the cane over to Yoko.

Yoko aimed for Chai's bald head and whipped the cane as fast as she could. Chai's head and face were no longer distinguishable. She stepped back and handed the cane to Nikki.

Nikki gritted her teeth as she struck out with the cane to lash at Chai's knees and legs, then she handed the weapon to Alexis, who walked behind the man to cane his thighs. She brought the weapon down twice before handing the cane over to Isabelle, who finished the job by caning the backs of the Chinese man's legs.

Isabelle handed over the cane to Julia, who shook her head and whispered, "There's no more flesh to cane." She handed the cane to Charles, who did his best not to look at the flesh and blood sticking to the bamboo strips. He tossed the cane to the ground and walked over to John Chai to inspect his battered body. He nodded to the women that it was time for them to leave. None of them needed to be told twice. They scurried quicker than the rats as they made their way out of the tunnels.

In the kitchen, they looked at one another, their faces shocked at what they'd just done.

"Tea, anyone?" Myra said.

"Screw the tea, Myra, we need something a little more substantial. Where's the hard stuff?" Myra pointed to the cabinet. Kathryn withdrew two bottles of hundred-proof brandy, and handed them around. "This is no time for social manners. Swig and pass the bottle around." They didn't sip, they gulped — even Myra.

"I never saw a skinned man before," Alexis said hoarsely.

"Is it going to ruin your life now that you've seen it?" asked Kathryn, tougher than nails.

Alexis took another gulp of brandy before she responded. "Not one little bit."

Julia's voice was quiet, conversational. "He could get a massive infection and die."

"Yes, that could happen, but it won't. Charles knows exactly what to do. Mr. Chai is being taken care of as we speak," Myra said. "However, the man will never be the same again. Now that we've exacted my vengeance, I want to thank you all for everything you've done to help me. Perhaps we should retire now."

"Is there anything I can do to help Charles?" Julia asked.

"No, dear, there is nothing for you to do. Charles has everything under control. Goodnight, girls."

Their eyes solemn, the women waved to Myra as she made her way to the kitchen staircase that led to the second floor. They started to chatter the moment their leader was out of earshot.

"Will the man die, Julia?" It was the question they all wanted to ask, but only Yoko voiced it.

Julia poked her finger into the dirt of her plant sitting under the kitchen skylight. She stirred the loose dirt and then added a quarter cup of water to the healthy plant. "I don't know, Yoko. If Myra said Charles has it under control, then I believe he does. I would imagine he has a large blanket that is spread with an antibacterial ointment. Mr. Chai will be given antibiotics and painkillers orally or perhaps by injection. I think the plan is to take him to a hospital in the next day or so after we . . . After we make a few suggestions."

Nikki nibbled on her lower lip. "It had better be damn quick then." At the women's questioning looks, she told them about Jack Emery's phone call.

"He's on to us," Alexis moaned, imagining life in a prison cell again. "My God, what are we going to do? Are you going to meet him? Why don't you want Myra and Charles to know?"

"I didn't want to spoil Myra's . . . She waited so long. I guess I thought Charles would call a halt and go after Jack himself. I don't know if I made a mistake or not. We need to make a plan, girls." The two brandy bottles continued to circulate around the kitchen table.

The ever-verbal Kathryn spoke up. "It sounds to me like Jack Emery has really pieced everything together. We can't pretend we don't know about it for your sake, Nikki. And let's not forget his friend Mark Lane."

All eyes turned toward Nikki. They waited. Her voice was cold and tight when she said, "I agreed to meet him to stall him so Myra could have her revenge this evening. What else could I do? Look, if you're worried about me, don't be. I know where my allegiance lies. I'll do whatever I have to do as long as we all agree."

Isabelle asked, "Are you still in love with Jack?"

Nikki leaned back in her chair. Her first reaction was to lie but then she answered truthfully. "Yes. But, that doesn't change anything. Jack is prepared to go to the authorities, and I belong to the group, so he won't bat an eye about turning me in if he has proof. But the operative word here is *proof*. Does he have any? I don't know. Is he blowing smoke? I don't know. He's got his theories and those theories are on the money. Sooner or later, someone in authority is going to listen to him. I'm surprised he hasn't gone to some newspaper reporter. I think we're safe until he does that. The flip side to that is then it's too late for all of us. So, let's spin this. I'll go with the majority."

Upstairs, Myra sat down on the top step and hugged her knees. Tears rolled down her cheeks. Murphy did his best to lick them away. Myra reached out to stroke the shepherd's head.

"Mom, you need to tell Charles."

"Oh, Barbara, is that you? Oh, thank you for . . . for coming to talk to me. I think about you every minute of the day. What is it you want me to tell Charles, dear?"

231

"You have to tell him about Jack and Nikki. Don't pretend you didn't hear what they were saying down there. Charles needs to know. By the way, you did good down there, Mom."

More tears rolled down Myra's cheeks. "Then why don't I feel better? We skinned that horrible man. Because he . . . he took you and your unborn child away from us. I'll be a murderer if he dies."

"He's not going to die, Mom. People like him live to ripe old ages. You were right about something, though. He's never going to be the same. His life as he knew it will never be what it was. His best hope is that he has some good memories to make his new life bearable. You need to go down to the tunnels and talk to Charles. We have to watch out for Nikki and the others. Jack Emery can ruin everything you're doing and planning on doing in the future. Are you listening to me, Mom?"

"Of course I'm listening, Barbara. Nikki still loves Jack."

"Yes, she does, but she's no fool, Mom. Our Nik is a bright girl. She'll try to do what's right. Trying might not be good enough, Mom. Don't waste time; go to Charles. I'm going to my old room to wait for Nik. I love you, Mom."

"I love you, too, darling girl. More than you can ever know. I'll do what you ask and talk to Charles."

Murphy nudged Myra's neck with his snout. Myra continued to stroke his big head as she ran the conversation with her dead daughter over in her mind. Did she dream it? Was it all the brandy she'd had in the kitchen? Or was it wishful thinking on her part? Maybe all of the above.

Holding on to the stair railing, Myra got to her feet, feeling a hundred years old, ancient, as she made her way down the long hallway that led to the spiral staircase in the middle of the house. She quietly made her way down the steps, Murphy at her side. She stopped at the bottom to listen. She could hear voices in the kitchen but she couldn't distinguish the words. She then made her way to the secret door, Murphy still with her, nudging her along.

Myra came to a stop when she reached the opening in the tunnel that led to John Chai's cell. All traces of what had gone on a short while ago were gone. Even the platter of food was nowhere to be seen. The bamboo cane and the CD player were also gone. Charles was leaning against the wall, staring into the cell where John Chai lay wrapped in a pristine white blanket soaked with a soothing antibacterial salve. His face and head glistened with the same antibacterial ointment. Myra thought he looked dead.

Murphy walked over to Charles and poked his leg with his snout. Charles continued to stare into the cell. "What is it, Myra?"

She told him all about Jack Emery.

"Ah, another problem. Well, I have all night to think about it. I want to stay here in case Mr. Chai tries to unwrap himself."

Myra's voice was bitter. "And if he does?"

"He could get an infection and die on us. That will make us murderers. We don't want that, Myra. We may be many things, my dear, but we are not murderers. Tomorrow evening he will be taken to a private hospital."

"That's it?" Myra asked in disbelief. For a moment she looked outraged.

"There's a little more to it," Charles said carefully. "My people will take over from there. At some point, Mr. Chai will be transported to England and from England back to his own country."

"And this never happened?" Myra said softly.

"And this never happened," Charles said just as softly.

"Was it just, Charles? Did we avenge our little girl? Are we going to be able to live with ourselves?"

Charles took so long to answer that Myra pressed his arm for a response. "Yes, Myra, it was just. Extreme, but just. We both have to accept the fact that nothing can truly avenge our little girl. She's still gone. Will we be able to live with ourselves? We might have a few bad moments from time to time, but yes, I think we will be able to. It's late, Myra. Go to bed and I'll sit here and think about our newest problem."

"All right, dear. I'll go to bed, but I know I won't be able to sleep. Goodnight." Myra leaned over to kiss Charles's cheek. Murphy woofed softly as he led the way out of the tunnel.

In the kitchen the girls were still talking. Myra headed for the main staircase. Suddenly she was so tired she could barely stand. She sat down on the fourth step from the bottom. Barbara and Nikki had slid down this staircase hundreds of times. She'd placed pillows at the bottom so they wouldn't hurt themselves. She herself had slid down the bannister on her fiftieth birthday, or was it her sixtieth? For the life of her she couldn't remember. But in the scheme of things, it wasn't important.

Myra leaned against the newel post and closed her eyes. She was asleep in an instant. Murphy tilted his head to the right and then to the left. When he was satisfied Myra was asleep, he stretched his body out on the third step, his big head on his paws. He didn't close his eyes though.

A long time later, when Myra's hold on the newel post grew lax and slipped, Murphy reared up and raced to the kitchen, where he tugged on Kathryn's pant leg, his signal that she was to follow him. She got up and ran after her dog, the others following.

Together the girls managed to get Myra upstairs to her bedroom. She mumbled and muttered but didn't wake up. Nikki covered her with a flowered quilt, turned on the night light and left the door ajar.

"Stay, Murphy," Kathryn ordered.

Murphy hopped on to the bed and scratched around for a few minutes before he settled himself at the foot. This time, he closed his eyes.

Outside in the hallway, Nikki turned to the others. "We'll meet in the kitchen at five thirty. Goodnight, everyone."

They each made their way to their respective rooms. No one said a word.

Seventeen

For hours Nikki watched the red numerals on the digital clock turn over. It was almost five o'clock. Time to get up, shower and meet the girls in the kitchen. All night long she'd let her mind go in all directions. She was no closer to knowing what to do about Jack Emery than she was when she went to bed hours ago. All she knew was that she was going to meet him at Mulligan's Café for doughnuts and coffee.

She'd never been a good liar. When she was a child, Myra had drummed into both her and Barbara that "The truth will set you free." Not this time, Myra. Not this time. The truth will land us all in jail with Jack Emery standing on the other side taunting us the way we taunted John Chai.

During the long hours of the night she'd toyed with the idea of asking Jack and his partner to join the Sisterhood. If she did that, it would be an admission of guilt. She still loved Jack, but she didn't trust him.

Just the way he didn't trust her. How sad this all was.

Nikki swung her legs over the side of the bed and headed for the shower. She looked back once to see if the rocker was moving or if Willie, Barbara's worn teddy bear, was where she'd left it. Everything in her bedroom looked normal. She felt sick to her stomach when she brushed her teeth.

Nikki was in and out of the shower within minutes. As she dressed for the day, she craned her neck to see what the weather was like outside. Darkness. Suddenly she wanted to cry the way she'd cried as a child when her problems seemed insurmountable. One last look in the mirror showed dark circles under her eyes. She shrugged. At least they would match her navy wool sweater and matching slacks. She wore no makeup. What was the point? She was almost to the door when she walked back to the small dressing table to spray perfume on her wrists and the lobes of her ears.

The room still looked normal. The rocker was still and Willie was right where she'd left him. Nikki closed her eyes for a second, hoping she'd hear Barbara's voice when she reopened them. It didn't happen. She was on her own. Shoulders slumped, she made her way down the hall and down to the kitchen.

Nikki blinked when her foot hit the last step. The girls were seated at the kitchen table, even Myra. Charles was serving breakfast. How had she not noticed the fragrant aromas?

"How . . . how's our . . . guest?" was all Nikki could think to ask.

Charles took a moment to look up from the grapefruit he was scoring. "Mr. Chai is resting as comfortably as can be expected. He's heavily sedated but his vital signs are stable. He isn't going to perish, if that's your next question."

Nikki reached up for the grapefruit. She wondered if she would be able to eat it. She tried, but in the end she slid it to the middle of the table before she reached for her coffee cup.

"Are you girls ready to hear our plan?" Myra asked as she gazed at Nikki. "The girls told me you were going to go to meet Jack Emery and then play it by ear. I'm afraid we need more of a plan. Charles thinks he might have a solution."

"I'm certainly all ears," Alexis said.

"We all are," Isabelle agreed.

"For starters," Charles said, "the roads are clear so driving is no problem. They are predicting several more inches of snow later this evening, but that won't interfere with our plans."

Nikki stared out of the kitchen window. The new day was just beginning. In another few minutes it would be blinding white outdoors. She gritted her teeth. "What are our plans, Charles?"

"It's fairly simple. I think it will work and give us a little time to whisk Mr. Chai away from these premises and Julia back to Switzerland. You will meet Jack, at which point you will comment that he looks like he's coming down with a bug of some sort. The power of suggestion. I'm going to give you a pill to drop in his coffee. How you will do that is entirely up to you." At Nikki's look of concern Charles hastened to add, "All it will do, Nikki, is to make him sweat, give him chills and a terrible, terrible headache. He'll think he's coming down with the flu. He'll want to sleep within ten minutes. You will be solicitous and offer to drive him home. Jack will have no other recourse but to accept your offer. However, you won't take him home, you'll take him to Marie Lewellen's house. Isabelle and Alexis, wearing minimal disguise, will go to Jack's apartment where, once inside, they will render his roommate,

Mark Lane, useless and then bring him to Marie Lewellen's house to join Jack. Any questions so far?"

Nikki looked around the table. The others were nodding their heads in approval.

"Kathryn, also in disguise, will play the part of a nurse and will stay with the two of them until it is safe for her to return to Pinewood. They will be so groggy and disoriented they won't have any clear memories of what transpired when they recover. No harm will come to either man. After Kathryn leaves, they will recover with nothing worse than a hangover for their ordeal."

Nikki groaned. She looked doubtful and voiced her concern. "Charles, how do you think I'm going to drop something in Jack's coffee without him seeing me do it? I know him. He'll be expecting something like that. I want you all to stop thinking he's a fool. He isn't. Right now he's angry. There are no rules when Jack gets angry. I just want you to know that."

"Jack will get a call from Mark. Of course it won't be Mark. He will have to walk toward the phone. That's when his back will be to you. That's when you drop the pill in his coffee. There will be static on the phone when he picks it up. He'll blame it on the storm. A lot of wires are down all over the area. It's the easiest and safest scenario I could come up with. I think it will work."

"And if it doesn't?" Nikki said.

"Plan B, dear. You don't want to know," Myra said cheerfully. "If I were you, I'd think about going back upstairs to put on some makeup."

"You would, huh? OK, Myra, I can take a hint."

The table cleared instantly as Alexis led the other girls to her room to work her magic. Nikki bounded up the back stairway and headed for her room.

Mark Lane looked at Jack as he shrugged into his down jacket. "You look like shit, Jack. Are you feeling all right?"

"I feel like shit, too. I think I'm coming down with a cold. My head is all stuffed up and I didn't sleep at all last night. That coffee I drank didn't help much either. Did you see my wool hat?"

"Yeah, Jack, I did see it. It's hanging out of your pocket. Are you sure it isn't just a case of the jitters at being up close and personal with Nikki again?"

"Yeah, that too. A double whammy. Look, I'll see you when I see you. If you come up with anything on that computer of yours in regard to that little sojourn to China, call me at Mulligan's. I need all the ammunition I can get to show Nik I'm not just fooling around."

"Good luck, Jack."

Jack offered up a sickly grin. "Where you been, Mark? Luck's my middle name."

A blast of arctic air slammed against Jack when he opened the lobby door of his apartment building. He did a double take when he saw his car stuck behind a snow bank. "Well, shit!" He stomped his way back upstairs and opened the apartment door. "We never shoveled out our cars, Mark! I'll have to call a cab."

"Oh, yeah, we were going to do that, weren't we? Sorry, buddy. You need taxi fare?"

Jack showed him his middle finger as he dialed the cab company. He marched back to the lobby again to wait for the cab. He realized then he felt worse than shit. He felt half-dead. He touched his forehead the way his mother used to do when he was a little boy to see if he had a fever. His brow felt cool to his touch. He barreled out the door when he saw the blue and white taxi glide to the curb. He had to stomp through the piled-up snow to get into the cab.

Snow immediately oozed down into his shoes. Shit! Cold wet feet meant he was *really* going to get sick.

Jack leaned back against the cracked leather seat and closed his eyes. He remembered two years ago when he'd gotten sick and Nikki had played nurse. She'd made him hot buttered rum drinks and chicken soup and nursed him around the clock. In the whole of his life he'd never felt so loved, so cared for. Somehow she'd convinced a doctor to make a house call, something unheard of in the District. She'd gone to the drugstore, picked up his prescriptions, set the timer on the stove to remind her to give him his medicine at precisely the right time. She'd even brought him fresh flowers to put on his nightstand. He wondered now if he would have died without her care.

And now he was preparing to repay that love and devotion by sending her and her friends to jail. There was something wrong with this picture.

"Hey, buddy, this is Mulligan's. You awake back there? That'll be seven fifty."

Any other time, Jack would have paid and given the driver a dollar tip. Today, he handed him a ten-dollar bill and said, "Keep the change." He hopped out of the cab and again had to step over a pile of snow. He slipped and went into the soft snow up to his knees. Cursing under his breath, he did his best to shake off the snow before he entered the steamy café.

Mulligan's was a small place with just nine tables with checkered table cloths and captain's chairs. The bar area was a lot of mahogany and brass with matching bar stools. At night, Mulligan's rocked, but the breakfast crowd were mostly older business types who were always in a hurry. They did a tremendous take-out business at this time of day. Jack was happy to see Nikki seated at a table across the room. A premium table. Pretty girls always got the best tables. He wished this was a date, but all the wishing in the world wasn't going to change what was happening.

"Hi, Nik. How's it going?"

"Hello, Jack. It's going. You know the law, busy, busy, busy. Are you all right? You look . . . *peaked*. Actually, Jack, you look sick."

He did feel sick. Physically sick and sick at heart. "Is that concern I hear in your voice, Ms. Quinn?" Sarcasm dripped from his voice as he shed his down jacket, wishing he could take off his wet shoes and socks.

"Believe it or not, Jack, yes, it is concern. Everyone I've come in contact with lately seems to have something flu-like. You need to take care of yourself. Sitting up in trees in the cold is not conducive to good health. Do you have a fever?"

"Cut the crap, Nik. Why the sudden interest in my health? So what if I'm coming down with a bug. What's it to you?"

"I'm sorry I asked. Let's cut to the chase here so you can go home and take care of yourself. I think you said you had me and my friends dead to rights or something like that. You're planning on turning us in to someone for something. How'm I doing so far? You have pictures of guests coming and going at Pinewood. What do you want from me, Jack?"

"The truth."

Jack looked up at the waitress who was holding a Pyrex coffee pot with an orange band around the rim. He shook his head. "I don't want decaffeinated, I want regular coffee and a bagel with cream cheese."

"What truth, Jack? Your truth or my truth?" Nikki steeled herself to try to look relaxed while an army of worms tore at her stomach.

"Why did you go to China?"

"What business is that of yours? I can go

anywhere I want. The last time I looked, I was of age. That means I do not have to answer to anyone. If you absolutely have to have an answer, I went to an engagement party. If you absolutely need to know the names of the engaged couple, I will be happy to email them to you. I'll even scan the invitation and send it along, too. Next question?"

Jack shifted in his chair. He could feel his feet sloshing inside his shoes. He felt cold and miserable. "Do that. My next question is, who's the old guy you brought back with you? This guy," he said, tossing a photo on the table.

Nikki picked up the photo and looked at it carefully. She handed it back to Jack and said, "I don't really know who he is. An old friend of Charles. He was sick. How is that any of your business?"

"Where is he now? I'm making it my business."

"I don't know, Jack. It's none of *my* business. But I'm going to take a wild guess here and say he was reunited with family members. For all I know he could be a terrorist intent on blowing us all up. That means I don't have a clue. Next question."

"The chick with the red bag. I know all

about her. What does she tote that bag around for? I have a dossier on her."

"Then you know Alexis Thorne is a client and she's off limits. Attorney–client privilege."

"C'mon, c'mon, she knows how to change people's appearances. She went with you to China and somehow you snatched John Chai. She doctored him up and you guys have him at Pinewood. Attorney–client privilege my ass."

Nikki burst out laughing. She hoped her laughter didn't sound as forced as it felt. Damn, when was Jack going to get that phone call? "Next question."

"What happened to Julia Webster? She used to be a regular visitor to Pinewood. I think the old lady, this woman," Jack said, handing a second picture across the table, "is Dr. Julia Webster. I think she was the cowgirl, too."

Nikki laughed again. She heard the phone next to the cash register ring. Thank God. A waitress approached the seated area.

"Is there a Jack Emery here?"

Jack stood up. "I'm Jack Emery."

"Phone call, sir. You can take it by the register."

Jack looked at Nikki and shrugged. She

shrugged in return. The minute Jack turned his back, she reached across the table for a sugar packet and then dropped the pill in her hand into Jack's cup. She signaled the waitress for a refill. While the waitress was filling Jack's cup, Nikki picked up half the bagel and bit down. Jack returned to the table, a frown on his face. "Damn phones aren't working properly. My cell isn't working, either. Can I borrow yours?" He slurped at his coffee while Nikki dug around inside her purse for her cell phone and handed it over.

"I think I forgot to charge it. You might have a minute or so."

Jack clicked it on. He looked disgusted. "It's as dead as mine." He took another deep swig of coffee.

"Maybe one of the phone booths out on the street will work. Are we finished here, Jack? Let's put all your cockamamie notions to rest once and for all. You have to stay out of my life, and Myra's too. Do you hear me, Jack?"

"Of course I hear you. I always listen to everything you say. You didn't answer my question about Julia Webster."

"Julia is a client, too. It's the darnedest thing, Jack. She disappeared without so much as a goodbye. She did pay her bill before she left. If you want my opinion, I think she couldn't take the embarrassment of her philandering husband so she just packed up and left. I read the papers just like you do, Jack. Are you sure you're all right?" Nikki asked, leaning across the table to peer closer at Jack. "You don't look so good."

Jack reached for a paper napkin and wiped at his face. The napkin came away drenched. "I guess I am coming down with something. Will you ask the manager if he can call me a cab?"

"I thought you said the phone wasn't working. Did you come here by cab?"

"Yeah, we . . . we kind of forgot to shovel out our cars."

"I can drive you home, Jack. Are you still in the same apartment, or did you move?"

"I moved in with Mark. Jesus, I can't remember the last time I felt this bad . . . It's like that time you took care of me. You know what, I'll take that ride if you don't mind."

Nikki put on her jacket and zipped it up. She waited and watched as Jack struggled to fit his arms into his bulky jacket. In the end, she had to help him.

"Maybe I should take you to the hospital, Jack. I don't mind, if that's what you want me to do. It's your decision."

"Damn, I can hardly stand up. You have to help me, Nik. No hospital."

Nikki dropped some bills on the table before she put her arm around his shoulders. She felt light-headed. He smelled so good, felt so . . . comforting. "Hang on to me, Jack. I'm parked right in front."

"I feel like a *wuss,* leaning on you like this."

"It's OK, Jack, you're sick. When you're sick, all the rules go out the window."

"Do you still love me, Nik?"

"OK, Jack, here's the car. Stretch out on the back seat. I'll have you home in bed before you know it."

"You didn't answer my question, Nik."

"I know."

Eighteen

Eight blocks away from Mulligan's Café, Alexis Thorne and Isabelle Flanders approached Mark Lane's apartment. Walking into the biting wind, they did their best to huddle inside their ratty, threadbare denim jackets. The minute they entered the spartan lobby, Alexis removed her wool cap to reveal a headful of phony dreadlocks. She looked dirty and unkempt, as did Isabelle. They looked like street people. Alexis opened her mouth to reveal a gap between her beautiful white teeth. She now looked snaggle-toothed, nothing like her normal self. She'd worked a full twenty minutes to change the shape of her mouth. The others had been more than a little impressed.

"OK, where's the damn paper?" she hissed. "Good thing this isn't a doorman building or we'd never be admitted. It's hard to believe we look as bad as we do. I'm freezing my butt off here; let's get this show on the road. They live on the third floor so let's take the stairs. No sense in inviting trouble by taking the elevator."

"Twenty-four C is their apartment," Isabelle said. "You do your thing, Alexis. I have the syringe. Julia said to shove it through his clothes and just aim for the general area of his ass. I'd like to know how we're going to get him to turn around. You look so *skeevy,* the guy isn't going to take his eyes off you even for a second."

"Look, Isabelle, just jab him wherever you can, because you're right, he's not going to want to give us the time of day. At best we'll have just a few minutes, if that. OK, here we are. Stay to the side so he can't see you through the peephole."

Holding a folded sheet of blank paper in her hand, Alexis stepped up to the door and rapped sharply before she leaped backward to do a jittery dance, her head lolling from side to side to some unheard music. She squinted and knew an eyeball was appraising her. She jiggled some more as she waved the folded paper this way and that. When the door opened, the chain intact, she said in her best Jamaican drawl, "Hey, mon, Jack sez to bring this over and you'd give me an Andrew Jackson. You got

Jackson, mon? Show me. C'mon, mon, I'm freezing out here. Don't you rich people believe in heat?" Alexis grinned, her artwork fully displayed.

"Jack who?" Mark said, eyeing Alexis suspiciously.

"Jack, thas all he sez, mon. Sez give to you, you give me twenny dollar. Show me Mista Jackson, mon, or I is leavin' here right now, mon. *Sheattt!* I knew the mon was puttin' me on." Alexis whirled around, the loose sole of one of her sneakers flapping on the tile floor as she headed for the stairs.

Isabelle heard the sound of the chain sliding back. She flattened herself against the wall as the door opened wider, the syringe in her hand ready to find its mark. "Wait a minute," Mark called from the doorway. "Where was Jack when he gave you whatever you have in your hand?"

Alexis kept going but called over her shoulder. "Over by Mulligan's."

"OK, OK, here's twenty bucks. Hand it over."

Alexis stopped and turned around. "You want it, mon, you come and git it. After you give me my twenny dollar."

Jack stepped through the doorway and took two steps forward before Isabelle jabbed the hypodermic syringe through his sweat pants.

"Son of a —" Isabelle caught him and, with Alexis's help, got him back into the apartment.

"He's already in la-la land so let's go through his stuff. We should take his computer and whatever files we can find. If you watch him, I'll take the stuff to my car. We can make this look like a *real* burglary if we try. Would you look at this place! These guys are slobs. Chinese cartons, pizza boxes, beer bottles. Don't guys know how to cook? Never mind. Watch him, Isabelle. If he moves, give him a good swat. That must be his jacket over there by the door. You'll have to put it on him."

Six trips later, Alexis had both Mark's and Jack's computers and printers, their DVD player and two televisions locked in the back of Myra's Lincoln Navigator. She spent another fifteen minutes emptying out drawers, throwing cushions and lamps around to make it look more like a break-in.

"Take their jewelry if they have any," Isabelle called out as she huffed and puffed, struggling to fit Mark's arms into his jacket.

Alexis raced through the apartment to the two bedrooms. She found two small leather cases with tie pins, cufflinks and watches. She stuck both of them into her baggy pockets. She poked her head into the bathroom, eyed the Water Pik massager and the two electric shavers. She pulled the plastic liner out of the wastebasket and dumped them into it.

"OK, let's go. I'm leaving the microwave. Too bulky to carry. He's not totally out, is he?" she asked, winded from her exertion.

"I don't know, Alexis. How are we going to get him down two flights of stairs? Maybe we should take him in the elevator. There doesn't seem to be much activity in this building. We can pretend he's drunk. Yeah, let's do the elevator. Oh, damn, wait a minute. Didn't this guy have a heart attack or something a while ago? I think Nikki said that. See if he has any medicine. If he does, bring it. I'll get the elevator."

"Damn, you are on the ball, Isabelle. I never would have thought about that. Go ahead, get the elevator and put it on hold while I check the medicine cabinet. You don't think that shot's going to hurt him, do you?"

"Julia said it was just something to make him relax. He's relaxed all right. We're breaking all kinds of laws here, you know that, right?"

"This is a hell of a time to worry about

that," Alexis called from the bathroom where she was inspecting the medicine cabinet. She threw all the prescription bottles into the bag and trotted out to the living room. She took a last look around before she closed and locked the door. Why did men live in such total disarray? Because they needed women to clean and pick up after them, she guessed. "Ha! That will be the damn day I clean up after some man," she snorted.

Alexis and Isabelle managed, by holding Mark up under the arms, to get him to the elevator, down to the ground floor and across the lobby. Outside, the wind drove them from the back, literally pushing them forward as they pulled and dragged Mark to the car. A middle-aged couple stared at them but Isabelle waved airily and made a drinking motion with her hand and mouth. The couple turned away, disgust on their faces.

Inside the car, with Mark in the back, Isabelle said, "Turn the heater up and burn rubber, Alexis. It must be ten degrees out there. So, how much medicine is he on?"

"Two bottles of something. Most of the stuff was old, outdated. Looked to me like cold prescriptions and antibiotics. You're supposed to throw away old medicine.

Look, stop worrying. Julia said Charles accessed this guy's medical records and whatever was in the shot won't hurt him. I wouldn't have gone along with it otherwise. Myra and Julia both demanded to see his records and they were OK with it. They said he's healthy as a horse. But this guy is just peripheral and doesn't even deserve this. He just had the bad luck to be friends with Jack Emery . . . Listen, get out the directions to the Lewellen house. I didn't know Myra had bought that house. Did you know that?"

Isabelle shrugged as she read out which turn Alexis was to take next. "Nikki told me. She said Mr. and Mrs. Lewellen worked all their lives for that little house. She said Myra couldn't bear for it to go into foreclosure. Who knows, maybe someday . . ."

"No, Isabelle, the Lewellens will never be able to return. Wherever they are, they have new identities and they're still grieving over the murder of their daughter. Marie has to live with the fact that she shot her daughter's murderer. Such is life. Crazy world we live in, huh?"

"Yeah, it is crazy . . . Alexis, I can't get John Chai out of my mind. We skinned him."

"Yeah, we did. Skin grows back. Barbara Rutledge and her unborn baby are *never* coming back. Get over it, Isabelle. Damn, this is a big car and hard to navigate."

Isabelle giggled. "Guess that's why they call it a Navigator."

Alexis pretended to swat her friend. "That's it on the right, isn't it? Must be, Nikki's car is parked in the driveway. How did Kathryn get here?"

"Car service."

Isabelle peered out the window to see if she could see any curtains or blinds moving in the other houses. "This might be a stupid question, but shouldn't we be worried about the neighbors who are probably watching us at this very minute? What if they call the cops?"

"Charles has it covered. Kathryn has all the paperwork if some Nosy Nellie comes around asking questions. In addition, she's just a phone call away from all of us. Will you please relax? You're starting to make me nervous, Isabelle."

"I'm a worrier. What can I say?" Isabelle said, hopping out of the car. Together they managed to haul Mark Lane out of the back seat and up the driveway. The garage door slid upward just as they reached it.

Nikki and Kathryn took over just as the huge door slid downward.

"Let's get this dude into bed. I made coffee," Kathryn said. At the look of disbelief on Isabelle's and Alexis's faces, she hastened to add, "Life goes on. This has to look like a normal operation. Coffee is normal. I didn't say you had to drink the damn stuff. All I said was I made coffee. Someone stocked the cabinets and refrigerator. The heat's on, too. Jack is sleeping soundly and should remain asleep for another six hours or so."

It took the four of them to undress Mark and put him in an old pair of Mr. Lewellen's flannel pajamas before they settled him in a twin bed across from Jack, who was snoring with gusto. Nikki unfolded a Batman quilt from the bottom of the bed and covered Mark. Jack was sleeping underneath a Spiderman quilt.

Kathryn offered up a nifty salute and said, "Sleep tight, little buddies." The others laughed as they made their way to the kitchen where Kathryn poured herself a cup of coffee.

Alexis held out the liner from the wastebasket. "Lane's medicine is in here. You better read the instructions."

"Don't have to," Kathryn said over the

rim of her cup. "They're just placebos with fancy names. Mark Lane doesn't need medication. He's a hypochondriac. Hey, if you don't believe me, here's his medical history, and don't even think about asking me how Charles gets his hands on stuff like this. For some reason, Lane's doctors humor him. Charles thinks he wanted to get out of FBI fieldwork and into computer programming for the Bureau. When he had that heart business — which wasn't even a heart attack — that was his ticket out of fieldwork. Don't worry, I'll make sure he takes his placebos. Now, what are you guys going to do?"

Nikki brushed at her hair with her fingers. "I'm worried about Jack. He was already sick when he came into Mulligan's. Don't give him anything else, Kathryn. Just hot soup and tea. Same for Mark. We've come too far to screw up now. Be sure to take Jack's temperature and if it goes over a hundred and two, call me. He's prone to pneumonia. I nursed him through a bad spell a few years ago so I know what I'm talking about."

Kathryn was about to say something smart and flip until she saw the genuine concern on Nikki's face. "OK. I'll watch him carefully. Look, if he takes a bad turn, I'll call nine-one-one. I know what to do."

Nikki twirled the ends of her hair with her thumb and forefinger, a sign she was worried. "I think I'll take his temperature before I leave. The rest of you, finish your coffee. I'll be right back."

Alexis snapped her fingers under Nikki's nose. "Earth to Nikki. We aren't drinking coffee, and we're leaving now. We'll see you back at Pinewood."

When Nikki returned to the kitchen, Kathryn was on her second cup of coffee. "Sit down a minute, Nikki. I need to ask you something. It'll just take a minute." Her jacket in hand, Nikki sat down, her eyes full of questions.

"I need to know how you can do this. You love Jack. I think it's the kind of love I had for my husband. It's eating you alive, isn't it?"

Nikki nodded. "Yes. Yes, it is. But . . . You would have to understand how close Barbara and I were. How much I loved her, how much I love Myra and Charles. They're my family. At the end of the day, Kathryn, your family is all you have. I was going to be the baby's godmother; Jack was going to be the godfather. I was as excited as Barbara was when she found out she was pregnant. You didn't know Myra back then. After . . . after Barbara's death, I watched her waste away to nothing. She wanted to die to be with her daughter.

"It was the worst time of my life. Charles . . . Charles did everything he could, but you can't make a person eat, you can't make them care. All she did was sit in a chair twenty-four hours a day with the television tuned to CNN. She was hoping to see a picture of the man who killed her daughter. To my knowledge, the network never showed even one picture.

"I agreed to all this because it just wasn't fair that John Chai got off free. I know I swore to uphold the law, just the way Jack did. We made some mistakes along the way and he got suspicious. One thing led to another and I had to choose sides. Some days, I regret the path I chose, because I know in my heart that Jack is the only man I'll ever love. Jack is . . . different. He will never recover if he has to send me to prison, but make no mistake, if there's a way for him to do that, he will. We can't let that happen. That's all I have to say, Kathryn. That probably wasn't what you wanted to hear, but it's the best I can do. I really gotta get going. They might need help at the farm. Is there anything you want me to say to Julia other than goodbye?"

"Nope, that's it. Take it easy, Nikki. Jack Emery isn't sending any of us to prison. That's a promise. Go on now before the roads start to freeze up. Call me if you get bored."

"Will do," Nikki said as she walked to the door. "Lock up after me."

"You know it," Kathryn said. She shot the deadbolt home the minute the door closed behind Nikki.

Kathryn walked back to the bedroom where Jack and Mark were sleeping. She looked at both men and then placed her hand on Jack's forehead. Cool. She sighed with relief. Her heart felt heavy when she stared at the only man Nikki said she could ever love. And yet she seemed to be fine about Jack's code of ethics that could send her to prison. Her eyes started to burn. At least Jack was alive. Maybe a miracle of some kind would happen and Nikki and Jack would find a way to be together again.

But Kathryn didn't believe that for one minute. If Jack Emery had his way, he would send them all to prison and not give it a second thought. Her eyes narrowed and her heart hardened. "Well, screw you, Jack Emery. This is one chick you ain't sending to prison. Or Nikki, or anyone else. If I have to, I'll take care of you personally. Sleep tight, boys."

Nineteen

Julia's goodbye was sad yet sweet as she hugged her sisters. She was teary-eyed but mindful of Alexis's warning not to let the tears destroy her makeup job. "I'm going to miss you all. I'm glad I was able to help in some little way. And thank you for the snowmobile, Myra. I'll carry that memory with me till I return at Christmas. Remember now, take care of my plant, and don't forget to give Kathryn a hug for me."

Another round of hugs and kisses and Julia was running toward the car that would take her to the airport.

"It's snowing again," Myra said quietly. "I do hope Julia's flight isn't delayed."

"I don't think there's going to be a problem, Myra. It's just flurries. She'll take off right on schedule," Nikki said.

"We seem to be in a bit of a quandary here, don't we? Our mission is finished, and yet it isn't finished. What should we do now?" Isabelle asked.

"We could play mah-jong or watch television," Yoko said.

"On a Sunday afternoon! Bite your tongue, Yoko," Nikki said. "I think I'll take a nap."

Alexis looked around the kitchen, which was spic and span. "Who's making dinner? If no one minds, I'd like to putter around out here. Myra really doesn't like to cook and Charles is busy. Is it all right, Myra?"

Myra looked around, a vague expression on her face. "Of course, dear. Whatever you want to do is fine. I think I'll visit with Charles for a little while. He must be very tired. And lonely. Perhaps I can spell him for a little while. I think I'll just pour the rest of the coffee into a Thermos to take with me."

As Myra made her way to the secret door, she could hear pots and pans rattling in the kitchen. A tiny smile tugged at the corners of her mouth and stayed with her until she got to the tunnels. She rang the bells so Charles would know she was on her way to visit him.

For the first time in her life, Myra read annoyance on Charles's face at the sight of her. She was taken aback and stammered a greeting. She knew something was wrong, she could sense it. "What is it, Charles?"

"It's nothing, Myra. Please, I don't want you down here. It's not good for you to keep seeing this man in his present condition." Charles led her farther down the tunnel, out of John Chai's earshot.

"Charles, I am not some namby-pamby female. I have every right to see this man anytime I want. It doesn't bother me to see him and it doesn't bother me that we did what we did. Now, I want you to go into the house and take a nap. You look exhausted. Don't argue with me, Charles, because it's an order. Alexis is preparing dinner and Nikki is taking a nap. Julia's gone. I rather imagine Yoko and Isabelle will be reading or watching television, which leaves me at loose ends. By the way, it's snowing again."

"I'm fine, Myra. I catnap. Little power naps work wonders. I really don't want you here."

Hands on hips, Myra looked up at her beloved. "I don't really care, Charles. I'm staying and you're going to take a nap. Why don't you tell me what's really wrong?"

"Several hours ago I went up to the war room to make a few phone calls. Su Zhow Li is dead. No, no, Chai's people didn't get to him. Li made his way to England and on his arrival he suffered a heart attack. It seems he'd been living on borrowed time for over a year. When we spoke in China he alluded to the fact that he wasn't a youngster anymore, but he never let on that his health problems were serious. My people are sending me a secure fax soon. He was a good friend. A very good friend. I'm glad he died in England. I think that's why he wanted to return. He spoke several times about going back there but I had the impression he meant sometime in the future. Of course I'm aware that we may have escalated his departure."

Myra stared into the dark cell where John Chai lay. "Will his death affect Mr. Chai's return to China?"

"Possibly. My people told me Li vaporized his house. The only thing that remains is a pile of ash. No rubble. The airstrip on his land is still intact. That's the good news."

Myra digested the information. "Go, Charles. You need to sleep in a bed for a few hours. You will smell a lot better if you take a shower. I don't want an argument, Charles. Go! I'll just sit here and watch Mr. Chai."

"Has Kathryn reported in?"

"Yes. Her patients are sleeping soundly.

Jack's fever has gone down a little. Mr. Lane just sleeps. Obviously, both men were exhausted. Kathryn said she is sick of watching soap operas and game shows. She's hungry for one of your meals." Charles allowed himself a small chuckle as he kissed Myra's cheek. "I'll be back in two hours."

"Yes, dear, two hours. Sleep well."

Myra sat down on an old hardwood kitchen chair. She hugged her arms to her chest. She debated taking one of the quilts down from its peg. Did the rats scurry up and down it? Were they sleeping in the folds? Rather than finding out, she rubbed at her arms. Her gaze stayed glued to John Chai.

How still he looked. The truth was, he looked dead. Was he asleep? She wondered if he was dreaming about his ordeal. She finally decided there would be no point in dreaming, since Chai was living the experience.

Myra got up and walked over to the cell. She was stunned to see that the man's eyes were wide open. He stared at her malevolently but he didn't speak. She wondered how much pain he was in. "You're not a very pretty sight, Mr. Chai."

"Thanks to you and those animals you

surround yourself with. My father will find you and kill all of you."

"Is that so? Do you have any idea where you are? Do you even know what day it is? Do you have even a clue as to what you look like? You look just like the monster you are."

"There are plastic surgeons who . . ."

"No, the plastic surgeon hasn't been born yet who could help you. Right now your body is one massive scab. Soon, you are going to start to itch. But you can't scratch. If you do, you'll get an infection. If that happens, you could die. Your recovery is entirely up to you. I don't see any harm in telling you where you are since you don't know. You're in Switzerland," Myra lied. "It's January twentieth. You've been with us for two months. And not a word has been leaked about anyone looking for you. I find that incredibly sad. Your loving family — the father you said would move heaven and earth for you — isn't even looking for you. I guess no one cares about you, Mr. Chai."

"You're lying! I am my father's only son. He will find and kill you. That's a promise."

Myra moved back to her chair and crossed her legs. She could have been discussing the weather. "No, that's not a promise. One should only make a promise if one is prepared to carry through. I warned you about that once before. When we send you back to your family — the family who is *not* searching for you — you will be a freak of nature. Little children will run and hide when they see how ugly you are. Young women will turn away because you will offend them. Your father will hide you in some godforsaken place to live out your days. That's what you have to look forward to, Mr. Chai."

"Lies! Everything you say is a lie!" Chai screamed but there was no conviction in his voice.

"Very well, have it your way. But remember one thing, John Chai. It was a group of women who brought you to this point. Women. W-o-m-e-n! When you arrive at that godforsaken place where you will live out your days, you will remember all of us and what we did to you. You will dream about us and you will think about us every waking moment as we move on with our lives. We'll be going to parties, weddings, eating wonderful food, making love with our partners, going to church, raising our children. We will *not* be thinking of you. And when you finally die, my daughter will be waiting for you on the other side."

John Chai screamed and screamed and screamed until he was hoarse. Myra laughed, a cruel and bitter sound.

Myra opened the Thermos and poured coffee into the cup. She leaned back and sipped at it. Her thoughts carried her back in time to a warm, sunny day when she watched Barbara and Nikki riding their ponies. She was snapping pictures of the laughing group as Charles led both giggling girls around the fenced-in pasture. "Look, Mom!" Barbara shouted as she stood up in the saddle. "No hands, Mom!" Wiry little monkey that she was, she didn't fall, to Charles's relief. Not to be outdone, Nikki wiggled backward and slid off the pony's rump. How they'd laughed that day. Myra made a mental note to look in the photo albums when she returned to the main part of the house.

"What else should we talk about, Mr. Chai? I'm trying to be hospitable here. Don't scream, though, that irritates me."

Myra poured more coffee into her cup before she moved the wooden chair closer to the cell door. "I think I'll tell you about my daughter, the daughter you killed. I'll tell you about her from the day she was born. I just want you to listen."

Myra heard harsh noises coming from the cell and knew Chai was cursing her in every language he knew. She was glad he was hoarse. "Well, here we go. Barbara was born on a bright, spring day. It was the happiest day of my life. She had the most marvelous head of curly hair. By the way, your hair will never grow back, Mr. Chai. You will be bald-headed like all your Chinese ancestors. I'm sorry, I digress here. Barbara weighed . . ."

Kathryn walked into the bathroom and plopped a curly gray wig on her head. She withdrew a pair of granny glasses from her pocket and stuck them over her nose. Cotton puffs went into her mouth to plump up her cheeks. Two white tooth caps went over her front teeth, giving her a buck-toothed appearance. Her baggy sweater with the padding made her look like she'd gained a good twenty pounds and was twenty years older. She didn't look anything like Kathryn Lucas.

She poked her head round the door of the bedroom to make sure both men were still asleep. She walked over to Jack and slid the thermometer into his mouth.

When she withdrew it, she was glad to see his temperature had dropped down to a hundred. That had to mean he was on the mend. Lane was sleeping soundly, curled into the fetal position.

Kathryn looked down at the watch on her wrist. Another thirty minutes before they were due for their medicine. She admitted to herself that she was starting to get nervous. The original plan had been to move John Chai the night before, but he was still at Pinewood. That meant she had to stay on here an extra day. It was already late in the afternoon and she hadn't heard yet if Chai was going to be moved tonight or not. All she wanted was to get out of here and back to Pinewood. Maybe the snow that was falling a little more heavily now had something to do with Chai's transfer. She wondered if she dared to call Pinewood.

Kathryn walked to the kitchen and then out to the garage where she opened the door. She dialed the main number at Pinewood. Isabelle answered.

"What's going on?" Kathryn demanded. "I'm getting cabin fever. Tell Nikki that Jack's temperature dropped to a hundred. He's going to be just fine. So, what do you know, if anything?"

"Not much. Julia left for Switzerland. We told her goodbye for you, hugged her and off she went. Nikki's taking a nap. Alexis is making dinner. Yoko and I were watching some crappy Ninja movie on television. She loves that stuff. Myra is in the tunnel with Charles. No one said anything about moving the fucker tonight. I'll call you back as soon as I know anything."

The two women talked a few more minutes before Kathryn ended the call and walked back into the house. More hours to kill. She turned on the television and started to watch the same movie that Yoko and Isabelle were watching.

"This sucks," she muttered.

In the bedroom, Jack Emery rolled to the side of the bed before he struggled to sit up. A wave of dizziness washed over him. He did his best to focus, but the room kept spinning round and round. He squeezed his eyes shut to try to ward it off.

Where the hell was he? He tried opening his eyes again to see if the world was still spinning. The room tilted, then righted itself. He opened his eyes wider. Directly in his line of vision was Mark Lane. Jack turned, then wished he hadn't as the room started to whirl. He shut his eyes as his arm snaked out to grasp the post on the headboard. This wasn't his room. He yanked at the Spiderman quilt. This wasn't his, either. He opened his eyes to see Mark snuggled under a Batman quilt. Something tugged at his memory. Where had he seen these quilts? On television? Online? Damn, he had to go to the bathroom. The only problem was, he didn't know where the bathroom was.

Jack struggled with his memory. He'd gone to see Nikki at Mulligan's. He'd felt sick when he left the apartment to meet her and then when he went outside, he'd gotten snow in his shoes and his feet were wet and cold. His mother always said that when that happened you got *really* sick. Well, shit, he was really sick, more proof that the mothers of the world knew *everything*. He felt his forehead. It felt warm to his hand. "I must have a fever," he muttered. Damn, he wished he knew where he was and where the bathroom was. But even if he knew, could he stand up to make it that far?

As he continued to struggle with his memory, Mark stirred and rolled over. He groaned and moaned before he settled back to sleep.

Jack stood up gingerly, his head swimming as he staggered toward the bedroom door. In the blink of an eye, he went down like a sack of wet noodles. He opened his eyes to see a pair of serviceable white shoes, the kind his mother used to wear, right in front of him. Nurse's shoes. Was he in a hospital? He remembered Nikki saying he needed a doctor and would willingly take him to the hospital. He thought he had said no. Did he say no?

"I have to go to the bathroom," he croaked.

"Back to bed, young man," Kathryn said sternly. "I will fetch you a urinal. Do not get out of bed again unless I am here to help you."

"OK, OK, but you'll have to help me. Who are you? Where is this place? Why is my friend here? What's wrong with me? How long have I been here?"

"So many questions! All in good time. Lie quietly and I'll be right back." Kathryn trundled off, coming down on her heels harder than necessary for effect. Where in hell was she going to get a urinal? She searched under the kitchen sink and came up with an empty tomato juice bottle. She quirked her eyebrow at the rather small opening, hoping that Jack Emery had a good aim. Back in the bedroom, she handed over the container and said, "We're rather short on supplies, so I had to improvise. Sick or not, if you miss, you clean it."

"What the hell!"

"There will be no swearing in my presence, young man. You will do well to remember that." Kathryn turned her back and walked toward the door. It sounded like Niagara Falls behind her.

"I'm done and I didn't spill it either. Now will you answer my questions?"

"I have to get your medicine ready, sir. Would you like some broth or hot tea?"

Would he? Jack closed his eyes as he tried to decide if he was hungry or not. He decided he wasn't. He shook his head. Big mistake. The room whirled and twirled.

"What the hell is wrong with me? Where is this place? Where's Nikki?" He gritted his teeth and squeezed his eyelids with his fingertips until his world straightened out.

"You were a very sick young man. Miss Quinn brought you here for me to nurse you since you refused to go to a hospital. I'm a nurse. You are in my home. You had bronchitis that turned into pneumonia. You've been here for two weeks. At one point you were so worried about your roommate that Miss Quinn went to check on him. He was just as sick as you, so she brought him here. Today your temperature finally went down to a hundred. You still have a little way to go before you can shovel snow. I feel very confident in telling you that you will recover. You do, however, need nourishment. Perhaps later you will consider some Jell-O or some broth. Now, take these pills with this orange juice."

Jack was too exhausted to argue. As he was drifting off to sleep something about the nurse and Mark tugged at his memory. Maybe when he woke up he could figure it out. Good old Nik. She must still love him to see that he got all this good care.

Twenty

Nikki leaned over to turn on the lamp beside her bed. She didn't have to look at the clock to know what time it was because she'd been staring at it for the past three hours. She never should have taken that two-hour nap earlier. Or maybe it was because she'd been too lazy to get up and turn the thermostat down. It was stifling in the room. She picked up Willie, walked over to the rocking chair and sat down.

"Ooof. Hey, sit on your own chair, Nik. Leave Willie, though."

Nikki obediently got up and moved over to her own rocker. "Isn't it a little late for someone from the spirit world to be visiting?"

"Shows you what you know, Nik. We never sleep. Stop being so upset. You know everything is going to be fine. Jack's recovering nicely. I just came from there."

Nikki threw her hands in the air. "What

do you do? Do you just flit from place to place? You know that old saying, stick your nose in other people's business and you have no one to blame but yourself if your nose gets chopped off. He's not going to give up. He'll keep coming back till he catches us or we make a mistake. Hey, how do you think your mom did with her revenge?"

"Well, it wasn't exactly a feel-good moment, but she had to do what she had to do. I thought it a fitting punishment. Mom's one of a kind. I just hope she can find some peace now. You should go downstairs, Nik. The ambulance will be here soon to take Mr. Chai to a private hospital. Don't you want to wish him bon voyage?"

Nikki looked over at the clock. Three hours past the witching hour. Three a.m. She got up to look out the window. "It's snowing pretty hard. I doubt an ambulance, even if it's an emergency, can get out here to the farm without a plow ahead of it. Maybe Charles will have to postpone his departure."

"No. The ambulance is a converted Hummer. Those vehicles can get through anything. Mr. Chai is leaving. You should go downstairs, Nik. Mom might need you.

She's about ready to split her gut. You know how she can get sometimes. I'll stay here with Willie. Go, Nik."

Nikki hitched up the bottom of her flannel pajamas and sprinted out of the room. She found Myra pacing and wringing her hands in the kitchen. "What's wrong, Myra?"

"What's wrong? I'll tell you what's wrong. Charles and I just had our first ever fight. Well, maybe it wasn't a fight, more like a . . . ripe discussion. As usual, I lost. He thinks he can bring Chai up here by himself. I wanted to help but he said no. I'd like it if you'd wake the girls and go down to the tunnel to help. He needs to . . . to yell at someone besides me. Put your slippers on, dear."

Five minutes later the group was on the way to the tunnel. Charles looked up, dismay on his face.

Nikki took the initiative. "This is *our* gig, Charles, and we'll take him upstairs. Alexis, bring the ironing board over here."

"The ironing board!" Charles exploded.

"Yeah, Charles, the ironing board. It makes a perfect gurney. He is sedated, isn't he?"

"Of course he's sedated. An ironing board! In a million years, I never would have thought of that. I was going to carry him over my shoulder."

"OK, girls, let's do it! We'll slide him right off the bed and on to the ironing board. Alexis and Yoko, hold the board steady. Isabelle and I will slide him off. Myra, you tie those sheets around him so he doesn't slip as we carry him up the steps."

"What do you want me to do?" Charles asked.

Myra turned around. A wide grin stretched across her face. "Watch what a group of women can do when they set their minds to something, dear. You also have to get out of the way so we can do what we came down here to do. Oh, and Charles, you need to . . . What's the word you spies use all the time? Ah, yes, sanitize this place."

Charles saluted smartly before he turned around so the others, especially Myra, couldn't see the wicked grin on his face.

At the bottom of the steps, the women looked at one another and then at the steepness of the stone steps. "Upper body strength is what we need here," Nikki said. "Can you do it, Yoko? I'm OK with my end. If you are, Alexis will go first, Isabelle will be behind me and Myra will bring up the rear. Swing him around, Yoko, and I'll go first since I'm taller. Lift your end as high as you can. Isabelle, you might have to help her. We can do this. On the count of three, up we go!" Nikki took a deep breath as she balanced the ironing board almost at shoulder level. "This guy isn't exactly a featherweight."

Eight long minutes later, Nikki gasped, "We did it! Alexis, make sure those battery-operated warming packs didn't slip. He has to stay warm. The ambulance will be heated but we don't want him getting a chill. He has to be alive and well when he leaves here."

Myra looked up at the security monitor over the kitchen door. "I can see the ambulance. I'm going to open the gates now. If anyone wants to say goodbye, this is the time to do it." The women ignored her. She reached up for the whistle and blew two sharp blasts. The guard dogs raced to the heated barn.

The two men who got out of the ambulance were big and burly wrestler types. They breezed into the kitchen, looked at the ironing board, then at the women. "Is this the patient?"

"Now that's a brilliant deduction if I ever heard one," Alexis smirked. The men ignored her as they shook out a large warming blanket that they draped over the ironing board.

And then they were gone.

Myra looked dazed. "I'll make tea," she said.

"Like hell you will," Isabelle said as she reached into the cabinet for the liquor bottles. "We have a problem, girls. We drank all the brandy during Myra's last tea-making episode. We're going to have to drink this fine old Kentucky bourbon that says it's over a hundred proof and *aged*. Whatever the hell that means." She tilted the bottle and took a healthy gulp before she passed the bottle around the table.

Before long, the bottle was empty and the women were as drunk as a bunch of skunks.

Charles eyed them for a long minute when he entered the kitchen. He tried not to laugh as he carried them one by one up to the second floor. Myra was the last. He bent over her chair, his nose almost touching hers. "I think it's time for bed, my darling. You are some kind of woman, Myra Rutledge."

Myra opened one eye. "Charles! Oh, I have so much to tell you. About my road trip with Kathryn. We're going to the

Truckers' Ball but we have to get suitable outfits. I don't want to embarrass Kathryn and her friends. Is . . . is it over, Charles?"

"It's over, Myra."

"I'm drunk, Charles. The girls didn't want my tea. I had to do what they wanted. You don't think I'm going to turn into a . . . a sot, do you? I think I like beer better. I do love you. You are my prince. My shining knight. My love for all time. I will marry you. The girls can be our attendants."

Charles laughed as he picked Myra up and slung her over his shoulder. "I hope you remember this when you wake up, my dear. I've been asking you to marry me for twenty-five years."

"Oh, I'll remember, Charles. Maybe we can get married at the Truckers' Ball."

Charles laughed so hard he almost dropped his most precious possession in the whole world.

Kathryn jerked awake when the cellphone in her pocket buzzed to life. She bounced out of her chair to go to the kitchen so her voice wouldn't carry to the two sleeping men down the hall.

"Charles! Is something wrong?"

"No, nothing is wrong. Our guest just

left. An ambulance will be picking you up in exactly forty-five minutes. They'll bring you here to Pinewood. Kathryn, this is crucial so listen to me. Sweep the house, clean everything you touched, even the handle on the toilet. Do not, I repeat, do *not* miss anything . . . Oh, I didn't know you were wearing surgical gloves. Julia gave them to you? Still, do as I say. When will your guests wake?"

"By morning. I'll be waiting outside for the ambulance. Is Murphy all right?"

"Murphy is fine. He's sleeping with Myra right now. He does miss you, though. Be careful, Kathryn."

Kathryn raced through the small house, wiping and shining everything she thought she might have touched. She had a queasy moment when she looked at the tomato juice bottle filled with Jack's urine. She did what she had to do and moved on. When she was finished, she stood in the middle of the floor and looked around, trying to recollect what she had and hadn't touched. She looked down at the gloves she was still wearing. Satisfied, she put her coat on and was about to leave when she remembered the thermometer and the case it came in. She carefully wiped it down and returned it to the medicine cabinet. She was still wearing the surgical gloves when she locked the door behind her and stepped outside.

Kathryn was stunned at how hard it was snowing. It was three thirty. She thought about her footprints in the snow. How much more snow would fall before Jack and Mark woke up in the morning? How quiet and still everything was. She shivered inside her warm coat. She was at the end of the walkway the minute she saw the low square lights of the Hummer. A heavy-set man got out, helped her in, and then he and another man carrying a strange-looking broom proceeded to obliterate her tracks. The first man held a small machine that blew snow in all directions. Kathryn watched, boggle-eyed.

Who *were* these people?

It was toasty warm in the converted vehicle. She opened her coat, stripped off the latex gloves and removed the wig, the cotton padding in her cheeks and the false teeth caps. Now she felt like Kathryn Lucas again.

"Home, James!" she said. When neither man responded, Kathryn leaned back in her seat and closed her eyes.

Mark Lane woke first. He rolled over and stretched. Then he sighed. He finally opened his eyes and looked around. He looked down at the Batman quilt and then across the room at Jack, who was snoring loudly.

"Jack!" he bellowed. "Wake up!"

"Wha . . . What the hell! What the hell's wrong with you, Mark?"

"Open your goddamn eyes, Jack, and look around. Where the hell are we? Oh, Jesus, now I remember. Those two guys! They said they had a message from you and wanted twenty bucks. I never saw the second one till he jabbed me in the ass. Are you awake, Jack? Are you listening to me? Get up! Holy fucking shit, where is this place? How'd we get here? How did you get here?"

Jack rolled over and then swung his legs out of the bed. "Will you shut the hell up for a minute? I need to think. I got sick at Mulligan's and asked Nikki to take me home. She wanted to take me to a doctor or the hospital but I said no. I couldn't even stand up. She had to practically carry me to the car. I didn't send anyone to see you. There was a nurse here. She gave me pills and a bottle to pee in. Man, she was one ugly woman. I know this place, but I don't know how I know it."

"We're wearing pajamas. Someone

dressed us. Look, there's my clothes. Yours are over there on the other chair. Did you hear me, Jack? Someone saw our . . . Oh, shit!"

Jack got up, surprised that he was no longer light-headed or dizzy. He walked around gingerly, Mark right on his tail as he made his way through the small house. "I know whose house this is. It belongs to the Lewellens. Son of a bitch! Those goddamn women outsmarted us!"

"So what else is new? It's not the first time, Jack. I think it's time we gave up on this shit. Every time you get a brilliant idea we get shot down by those *women*. How the hell did you fall for it?"

"Fall for what? You saw me, I was sick as a dog when I left the apartment. I just got sicker and Nik . . . Nik . . . drove me home."

"Does this look like home to you, Jack? She brought you here."

"Then how did you get here, smart ass?"

"That grungy guy with the dreadlocks must have brought me here. See, it was a plan, and Nikki was in on it. We're here, so don't even think of disputing my theory."

Jack sat down on one of the kitchen chairs. "Make some coffee, Mark. Jesus, look at all that snow! And we don't have a car. How the hell are we going to get out of here? Wait a minute, where's the damn nurse?"

"You mean the nurse in your dreams? How the hell should I know? I never saw a nurse. It might be a good idea to find out what day today is. Is there a television or radio anywhere? What about a phone?" Mark asked as he filled the coffee pot with water.

A small ten-inch black and white television sat on the kitchen counter. Jack turned it on. "We've been here for three days and nights — four, if you count today," he said, his voice full of awe. "They needed all that time to . . . to . . . to do something. They had to get us out of the way. We're fools!"

"Watch it with that *we* stuff."

"I wasn't the one who let some *scuzzball* shoot a drug in my ass — you were. If you were that dumb you deserve whatever you got," Jack snarled.

"Oh, no, you were just the guy who let an old girlfriend work her magic on you. Five bucks says she drugged your coffee or whatever you were drinking. Then she plays Florence Nightingale and brings you here. How'm I doing, Jack? Talk about dumber than dumb."

"All right, all right, you made your point. But where's the nurse? When did she leave?" Not bothering to wait for an answer, Jack ran to the front door and opened it. There wasn't a footprint or tire mark to be seen. He ran to the garage door and opened it. No footprints, no tire marks. "Did she fucking fly out of here or go up the chimney?" he bellowed.

When Jack returned to the kitchen, Mark was leaning against the doorframe, coffee cup in hand. "They snookered us, Jack. We've been out of circulation for three days. This is just my opinion, but I would guess the nurse, and I use the term lightly, left after she drugged us up for the night. There's at least ten inches of snow out there and it's still falling. We're grounded, buddy."

"Yeah, looks like it. This isn't the end of it, Mark. Far from it."

"Famous last words, Jack."

Twenty-One

A wet, freezing snow — in fact more sleet than snow — was cloaking the arthritic-looking trees in the English countryside. Inside the house, which doubled as a private hospital, a doctor and nurse, both dressed in sterile white, looked out the window, their eyes full of concern at the weather conditions. In the background, shrill screams and curses could be heard.

The doctor-nurse medical team never speculated or gossiped about their patients. They did, however, discuss medical issues. For the first time in three decades, the nurse looked up at the doctor and said, "I can't wait till he leaves. He's driving me insane with his screams. You'll have to have me committed if the plane can't leave tonight."

The doctor's face was grim, his lips pressed into a tight line. "They'll be committing two of us if the flight is cancelled. He should have quieted down an hour ago.

He's fighting it and it's working to his disadvantage."

The heavy-set nurse, who had huge breasts, steel-gray hair and a ferocious expression, stomped her foot in anger. "Christmas is in two days. I want to spend the holidays with my family. The man was supposed to leave a week ago. They made a promise to us."

The tall, slim doctor's face took on an expression of annoyance. "We're healers, Maxine, not killers. He hadn't shed all his scabs last week. His new skin needs to be treated. He's screaming and cursing us because he itches. We'd be doing the same thing if we were in his position. The truth is, I doubt either one of us could deal with what that man is dealing with. I know I would be a raving lunatic by now. He refuses to accept the fact that we're helping him."

The phone behind the couple began to ring. They looked at one another before the doctor walked across the room to pick it up. "Hospital," he said curtly, and then listened. He gave the nurse a thumbs up, meaning the patient would be leaving as scheduled.

The doctor broke the connection. "It seems our employers found a daredevil pilot who is willing to transport our patient. For a huge sum of money, I might add. Someone will be here to pick the poor guy up," he looked down at his watch, "in exactly one hour from now. I have to get his paperwork ready and then I'll help you to dress him. They want him unconscious when they arrive. We have to work quickly, Maxine."

"Where . . . where are they taking him? Do you know?" the nurse asked.

The doctor looked up from the papers he was shuffling on his desk. "I don't know and I don't care. Nor should you. We've kept the man alive. He's virtually healed, which means we did what we were supposed to do. If you want my guess, I'd say he's headed for his homeland, China, and we're headed home for the holidays."

That was the most personal conversation the medical couple had ever had in their long years of service together for Her Majesty.

John Chai struggled with the restraints that bound him to the narrow hospital bed. He stopped cursing and shrieking long enough to stare at the nurse in her starched white pants outfit. "Give me something to stop this itching! I demand that you help me. What kind of medical person are you, you fat pig?"

"I'm the kind of fat pig who is not going to give you anything to stop your itching. You need to be quiet. I suspect you've already harmed your vocal chords. Be a good lad and lie quietly and the itching will lessen."

"If it takes me the rest of my life I will find you and kill you. You and all those women who did this to me. Do you hear me, you fat pig?"

"Yes, I do hear you. You don't even know where you are or where you've been. So, how are you going to go about this?" the nurse asked as she opened the locked medicine cabinet.

"It doesn't matter. I'll find you. My father's people will find you. I never forget a face. I will kill you."

The nurse turned around, a hypodermic in her hand. She tapped the top of it. A small squirt of liquid shot out. "You big silly," she said, a smile on her face. "You can't scare me."

"Then you're a crazy old fool. All women are fools. I'll get even with every last one of you. That's what you have to look forward to."

"If you don't lie still, this *will* hurt. It's your choice."

John Chai closed his eyes. He'd had enough pain. They weren't killing him, and the nurse told the truth when she said they'd kept him alive. That had to mean that at some point he was going to be freed. Then it would be his turn for retribution. The Americans had a saying. What was it? He struggled to remember as the drug started to take hold. Oh, yes. What goes around, comes around.

The nurse stood by the gurney in the entrance hall but her eyes were on the doctor who waited by the window, a manila envelope containing John Chai's identity papers in his hands. There were two sets of papers — his real ones, under the name of John Chai, and a new set, compliments of Charles Martin's people. Chai had left China under the name of Gan Jun and was returning under the same name. When he reached his final destination, he would be carrying his real papers, which would not show any entry or exit stamps of any kind. Further proof that he'd never left his country.

The doctor moved quickly. "The ambulance is here, Maxine. Our car is right behind. It looks like you'll be able to go to that sale at Harrods after all."

The nurse sighed. Until now, she hadn't actually believed the ambulance would ever arrive. She took a quick look around. "Doctor, where is the package that Mr. Jun arrived with?"

"Good Lord, I almost forgot about that." The doctor sprinted over to a cabinet that contained office supplies and withdrew a package wrapped in shiny silver paper and a huge red velvet bow. A Christmas present, he surmised. He was glad he didn't know the contents, for he was certain it wasn't the kind of present he and Maxine would put under their Christmas trees. He placed it at the foot of the gurney.

A blast of freezing air swept through the foyer. Two men dressed in heavy white snow gear entered, handed over a sheet of paper that the doctor scanned before he scrawled his signature at the bottom. He in turn handed over the manila folder and then pointed to the silver package. "Don't lose that in transit. I think it's important." Both men nodded as they wheeled the gurney through the doorway and down the path leading to the ambulance.

The nurse shut the door and said the same thing that she'd said thousands of times over the years when a patient left their hands. "Is the house secure, Doctor?"

The doctor responded to the question the same way he'd always responded. "The house is secure, Maxine."

The old nurse looked up and twinkled. "Then let's burn some rubber, Doctor. Harrods and my personal shopper are waiting for me."

Fourteen hours later, a cute-as-a-button Chinese nurse with an infectious smile wheeled her patient through Chep Lap Kok airport to customs. People stared and she smiled. She handed over her passport as well as Gan Jun's. She giggled like a schoolgirl when the attendant moved the gurney to lead the way the moment the Christmas present, still at the foot of the gurney, was X-rayed and the gurney searched. In less than ten minutes, the gurney was loaded into a private ambulance. It roared off, sirens wailing.

John Chai slept soundly as the driver raced to the countryside. On their arrival, the gurney was wheeled into the simple farmhouse. John Chai was transferred to a comfortable bed and covered with a thick down comforter. His papers, along with a wad of money secured in his own personal money clip, were placed on a wobbly nightstand along with the gaily-wrapped package. A fresh set of clothing, a shaving kit, toothbrush and cologne were placed in the makeshift bathroom. Enough food and drink to last three full days were in a cooler in the small kitchen.

The little nurse, who wasn't really a nurse, stripped off her latex gloves and stuck them in her pocket. "We're secure, Billy. Time to leave. We have some calls to make. Mr. Chai will sleep around the clock. When he wakes he will have a major headache but will be none the worse for wear. By that time, I'll be back in Washington and you'll be back in New York."

The hospital attendant, who wasn't really a hospital attendant, grinned. "Is it true the man hasn't seen a mirror since his . . . accident?"

The nurse shrugged. "I would assume that to be true since we were told to dispose of all mirrors when we rented this house. If you notice, there are no mirrors around. I just follow orders like you do. Personally, I couldn't care less. It's time to go, Billy."

The private ambulance was now transformed into a fish truck complete with decals on both sides. The drive back to Chep Lap Kok airport was uneventful as the nurse made call after call on her cell phone. At the terminal, Billy wiped down the fish truck. They separated when they reached the terminal.

Neither agent looked the way they had on their arrival just a few short hours ago. Billy was dressed as a cleric. The young nurse was now a schoolgirl, complete with white socks, glasses, a ponytail and carrying a colorful backpack on her shoulders. She skipped along, following the crowd, blowing bubbles with the gum she was chewing.

John Chai was back in his homeland.

"Oh, this is so beautiful," Kathryn said, as she eyed the elegant table in the dining room. "And the house smells heavenly. It's all so perfect, Myra. I think I speak for all of us when I say thank you for everything. I don't know what else to say. I never had friends like all of you."

Myra's cheeks pinked up as she held out her arms to the small group of women who were now like daughters to her. "Merry Christmas to all of you! And there is no need for thanks. It is I who should be thanking you. And I do, from the bottom of my heart. Now, if you're all as stuffed as I am from Charles's wonderful dinner, let's adjourn to the living room and that beautiful tree you all helped to decorate. Charles has a bottle of 1920 Dom he wants to share with all of us. And then I want to take some pictures of our little group. I knew you were all beautiful, but tonight proves it. You all glow and sparkle. Everything is so festive. You all look so festive."

Julia laughed, a genuine sound of mirth. "I think you're trying to tell us something, Myra. We don't exactly glow and sparkle when we're in our work duds, and you're right, we dressed up for you and Charles. It was the least we could do after all you've done for us. Christmas is always so special at Pinewood and it brings out the best in all of us."

"Let's get to that Dom and the presents," Nikki called out.

"You haven't changed a bit, darling. You and Barbara used to say the same thing when you were little. I always wanted the formality of a drink, wine for Charles and myself and Shirley Temples for the girls. It never worked."

"It's not going to work this year either, Myra. Charles plays Santa and hands out the gifts. C'mon, girls, hike up those long, glittering skirts and take your places by the Christmas tree," Nikki said gaily.

They were like little children, even Myra, as they all picked a spot around the twenty-foot balsam tree and sat down. Charles, wearing a Santa hat, clicked his camera again and again before he set the timer and crouched down in the center of the women. "I'll have copies made for everyone. Now, I must complete my duties and hand out the presents. Merry Christmas, everyone! May we have many, many more just as happy as this one!"

They laughed, they cried, they poked and prodded one another as the gifts were opened. It was Alexis and Isabelle, however, who held the spotlight. Alexis wept when she opened a small square box that held a set of keys and the deeds to the house she'd lost when she went to prison.

"Isabelle described the inside of your house and Charles and I did our best to duplicate it. I know, I know, there's one thing missing. Murphy!" Myra called. "Please bring in our guest!"

A golden blur streaked across the room and literally sailed across a pile of presents to land in Alexis's lap.

"Grady! Oh, my God! It is you! You didn't forget me!" She looked up, her eyes full of tears. "How . . . Why . . . Oh, you dear, sweet people. Isn't he beautiful? I never thought . . . How?"

"We lucked out, dear. The officer who took him when you went to prison is being transferred. He wanted to give him back to you but didn't know where you were. We've had him for a whole week," Myra said, tears rolling down her cheeks at Alexis's happiness.

"Isabelle, it's your turn," Charles said, handing over a long, tube-shaped present.

Isabelle tore at the gold wrapping and opened the tube. "It's . . . it's my license! How?"

"Shhh. The *how* isn't important. You've been reinstated. Congratulations!" Charles said.

"Now, I think we're ready for the Dom. I'll get it," Myra said, heading for the kitchen. "Charles, take more pictures."

In the kitchen, Myra set the crystal flutes on a silver tray.

"Way to go, Mom. You're some kind of Santa Claus. Merry Christmas, Mom."

"Oh, Barbara, now my Christmas is complete. How I wish you were here. I bought you a bright yellow snowmobile."

"I know, thank you. I was riding with Nikki when the girls took them out. That was so much fun. You look wonderful,

Mom. I mean you look happy and con-
tented."

"Life isn't perfect, dear, but, yes, I'm happy and contented. I miss you terribly. Will you stand by me at the piano when we start to sing the carols? Nikki is going to play."

"I'll be there, Mom. I'm always close by. Go ahead, they're waiting for that bubbly."

Myra reached up as she felt something touch her cheek. Had she felt a stray breeze from when Charles opened the kitchen door? Or did her dead daughter kiss her cheek?

"We're waiting, Myra. I thought you got lost out here."

Myra smiled when she heard her daughter's light laughter. Her first Christmas kiss. She looked up at Charles. "The only place I ever get lost is in your arms, dear."

"Now, that, old girl, is the best news I've had all day." He patted her rump as they sashayed their way back to the living room.

The others were waiting by the piano. Nikki was flexing her fingers. "This is the way we do it at Pinewood. First comes 'Silent Night,' then, 'O Come All Ye Faithful' and we wind up with 'Jingle Bells.' If you don't know the words, pretend you do."

★ ★ ★

Outside in the cold, Jack Emery stood behind the electronic fence. He could hear the piano and the sound of the Christmas carols. He'd never felt more lonely in his whole life.

"Merry Christmas, Nik," he said in a husky, choked voice.

Thousands of miles away, in a rural farmhouse, John Chai prowled about like a caged animal. His new skin shivered in the cold, so he quickly dressed in the clothes that were laid out for him. He saw the Christmas present and the manila folder at the same time. He quickly shuffled through the papers and money, stunned to see that they were all in his name. He stuffed everything back inside the envelope before he turned to the glittering package. He opened it cautiously. The only thing in the box, nestled in among the folds of tissue paper, was a mirror. He picked it up and looked at himself.

His scream thundered in his ears.

Epilogue

The women arrived one by one, each with a bouquet of spring flowers for Myra. As was their custom, they high-fived each other and then hugged Myra and Charles. It was the end of the April showers that would bring all the beautiful May flowers to the countryside. The women's light-hearted attitudes and spring attire matched the colorful flowers they held in their hands. Lunch today was being served on the terrace, with Myra and Charles presiding.

Grady and Murphy, fast friends these days, romped and played on the newly mown lawn. Their owners looked on, indulgent expressions on their faces.

"The good news, girls, is that Julia's condition is a tad better after that setback she had in February. She can tell us herself how well she's doing. Her doctor's last call was more than positive. So, let's make a toast to Julia and her well-being. And, somehow, Charles managed to get us a batch of soft-shelled crabs, the first of the season. I want a toast now. With gusto, girls!" Myra said. The women obliged, laughing and teasing as they drained their glasses.

"Where are the guard dogs, Myra?" Isabelle asked.

"In the barn. They only come out if they sense a threat. Charles and I felt it best to keep them on duty even though we weren't . . . ah . . . active."

"Wise move," Isabelle said.

Alexis looked at Nikki. "Any news on Jack Emery?"

Nikki's hands clenched into fists. "No. I haven't heard from him. However, he did send me a Christmas card." She waved her hand over her head. "I'm sure he's out there somewhere and knows we're all here. And I'm sure that, in his eyes, we're up to something. Can we get past Jack and his obsession? If we stay alert and on our toes, he will not pose a problem. If you're worried I'm going to waffle, get over it, I'm not. I hope we don't have to have this conversation again."

The women eyed one another. Their expressions showed they understood that Nikki was pissed to the teeth. Charles opened the door and walked out on to the terrace carrying a large platter.

"Ta da! Ladies, you are about to partake of the first soft-shell crabs of the season. Enjoy! By the way, Myra made the salad with our new lettuce from the greenhouse. Everything in the salad is organic. Eat heartily, ladies, because we have serious business to discuss later."

When the salad bowl was empty, the last crumb gone from the platter, Charles fired up his pipe and leaned back in his chair to gracefully accept the comments that made him smile. They made small talk, catching up with each other's activities since New Year's.

"The best part is, Julia's plant now has a trailer stem. With *nine* new leaves! It's thriving, just the way Julia is thriving." The women clapped their hands in approval.

Julia beamed. "I've never been happier and I can't ever remember when I felt this good." She looked around the table at the others. "I'm also mindful that I'm an experiment and it can go sour on me. I don't dwell on it but it's always there in the back of my mind. When I come back in June, after the last series of treatments, I want to be able to do my share, so I'm asking all of you if you can wait until I get back for the next mission. I don't mean we shouldn't pick a name at this time; we should. I'd just like to be able to be part of the team again."

The women nodded their agreement.

Charles tapped his pipe on the railing. "It's time, ladies." Chairs were pushed backwards as the women got up, their faces alight with excitement, to follow Charles and Myra indoors. Murphy herded Grady forward, growling lightly when the golden dog dawdled a little too long for his liking.

Inside the war room, the women took their seats. Their light-hearted mood changed instantly as they stared upward at the scales of justice on the monitor. This time the heavy table was bare except for the shoebox sitting in the middle.

"Alexis, pick a name," Myra ordered.

Alexis sucked in her breath as she reached inside the box to draw the small square of paper. Without looking at it, she handed the slip to Myra.

Myra unfolded the square and looked around the table before she read off the name. "Nikki!"

Nikki squeezed her eyes shut to ward off the dizzy light-headedness that threatened to engulf her. Somehow she managed to smile and look excited, but her mind was on Jack Emery.

Charles stepped down from his perch above them. "Now that we know who our next candidate is, I have something to share with all of you. I have here in my hands articles from the *Asia Times*, the *Hong Kong Commercial Daily*, the *Ming Pao Daily News*, the *Oriental Daily News*, and the *International Herald Tribune* — the English version. I'll pass the articles around to you but they all pretty much say the same thing, with the exception of the *Tribune*.

"It seems Mr. Chai, our former house guest, was picked up by the Hong Kong police. He spun a tale so bizarre sounding, the authorities called in the equivalent of our FBI. Mr. Chai spoke of a group of American women who kidnapped and tortured him. The only person who appears to believe Mr. Chai is his father, who promised deadly retribution in swift order. Mr. Chai named names and offered up descriptions, but the paper didn't publish them. The *Tribune* carried it a step further and interviewed Chai's two friends, Wing Wu and Quon Zheyuan, as well as the La Ling sisters. They scoffed at the story of Chai being abducted. The La Ling sisters said they left the private party with the American women and the three men were passed out cold from too much liquor. The *Tribune* went on to say something *did* happen to John Chai, as he had been caned and skinned and was left scarred from head to toe. It should be noted that Wu and Zheyuan have not been seen or heard of since they gave their initial interview. The La Ling sisters have not offered up any further interviews either, and remain behind a walled garden with their parents."

"Do the articles mention where Mr. Chai is now and what he's doing?" Myra asked.

"Just that he's in seclusion," Charles said cheerily. "The *Tribune* investigated a little further and found out that Mr. Chai had no exit or entry stamps on his passport, which should lead readers to believe that he concocted the story and was caned by a jealous husband in his own country. The *Tribune* speculated that Chai concocted his story because of a guilty conscience in regard to the tragic accident he had while living in the United States. The *Tribune* did not mention names. Do any of you have any questions?" When no one posed a question, Charles continued, "In that case, ladies, I think we can close our files on Mr. John Chai."

Myra raised her head slightly and then tilted it to the side as though she were resting her cheek on something. A gentle smile spread across her face.

"The case of John Chai has been completed. We will never speak of it again. I suggest we adjourn to the terrace so we can make a toast to another successful mission," Charles said.

The seven women nodded their heads solemnly as they filed out of the room.

John Chai, Barbara Rutledge's killer, now belonged to the past.

About the Author

Fern Michaels is the *New York Times* bestselling author of *Picture Perfect, Weekend Warriors, Payback, The Real Deal, Kentucky Rich, Plain Jane, Yesterday,* and many other novels. She shares her 300-year-old South Carolina plantation home with her six dogs and resident ghost, Mary Margaret, who leaves messages on her computer. Visit her at www.fernmichaels.com.

The employees of Thorndike Press hope you have enjoyed this Large Print book. All our Thorndike and Wheeler Large Print titles are designed for easy reading, and all our books are made to last. Other Thorndike Press Large Print books are available at your library, through selected bookstores, or directly from us.

For information about titles, please call:

(800) 223-1244

or visit our Web site at:

www.gale.com/thorndike
www.gale.com/wheeler

To share your comments, please write:

Publisher
Thorndike Press
295 Kennedy Memorial Drive
Waterville, ME   04901